One
Good Story,
That One

OTHER BOOKS BY THOMAS KING
PUBLISHED BY THE UNIVERSITY OF MINNESOTA PRESS

*The Inconvenient Indian: A Curious Account of
Native People in North America*

A Short History of Indians in Canada: Stories

The Truth About Stories: A Native Narrative

One Good Story, That One

STORIES BY
Thomas King

 University of Minnesota Press
Minneapolis

Originally published in 1993 by HarperCollins Publishers Ltd.

Published in 2013 in the United States by the University of Minnesota Press

Published by the University of Minnesota Press
111 Third Avenue South, Suite 290
Minneapolis, MN 55401-2520
http://www.upress.umn.edu

Library of Congress Cataloging-in-Publication Data
King, Thomas, 1943–
[Short stories. Selections]
One good story, that one : stories / Thomas King.
ISBN 978-0-8166-8978-1 (pb : acid-free paper)
I. Title.
PR9199.3.K4422063 2013
813'.54—DC23
2013027014

Printed in the United States of America on acid-free paper

The University of Minnesota is an equal-opportunity educator and employer.

30 29 28 27 26 25 24 23   10 9 8 7 6 5 4 3

For my brother, Christopher,
who knows why I got the
car and how late the
bowling alley stayed open.

Contents

One
Good Story,
That One

Alright.

You know, I hear this story up north. Maybe Yellowknife, that one, somewhere. I hear it maybe a long time. Old story this one. One hundred years, maybe more. Maybe not so long either, this story.

So.

You know, they come to my place. Summer place, pretty good place, that one. Those ones, they come with Napiao, my friend. Cool. On the river. Indians call him Ka-sin-ta, that river, like if you did nothing but stand in one place all day and maybe longer. Ka-sin-ta also call Na-po. Napiao knows that one, my friend. Whiteman call him Saint Merry, but I don't know what that mean. Maybe like Ka-sin-ta. Maybe not.

Napiao comes with those three. Whiteman, those.

No Indianman.

No Chinaman.

No Frenchman.

Too bad, those.

Sometimes the wind come along say hello. Pretty fast, that

one. Blow some things down on the river, that Ka-sin-ta. Sometimes he comes up too, pretty high. Moves things around, that Ka-sin-ta.

Three men come to my summer place, also my friend Napiao. Pretty loud talkers, those ones. One is big. I tell him maybe looks like Big Joe. Maybe not.

Anyway.

They come and Napiao, too. Bring greetings, how are you, many nice things they bring to says. Three.

All white.

Too bad, those.

Ho, my friend says, real nice day. Here is some tobacco.

All those smile. Good teeth.

Your friend Napiao, they says, that one says you tell a good story, you tell us your good story.

They says, those ones.

I tell Napiao, sit down, rest, eat something. Those three like to stand. Stand still. I think of Ka-sin-ta, as I told you. So I says to Napiao, Ka-sin-ta, in our language and he laugh. Those three laugh, too. Good teeth. Whiteman, white teeth.

I says to them, those ones stand pretty good. Napiao, my friend, says tell these a good story. Maybe not too long, he says. Those ones pretty young, go to sleep pretty quick. Anthropologist, you know. That one has a camera. Maybe.

Okay, I says, sit down.

These are good men, my friend says, those come a long ways from past Ta-pe-loo-za. Call him Blind Man Coulee, too. Ta-pe-loo-za means like a quiet place where the fish can rest, deep quiet place. Blind man maybe comes there later. To that place. Maybe fish.

Alright.

How about a story, that one says.

Sure, I says. Maybe about Jimmy runs the store near Two Bridges. His brother become dead and give Jimmy his car. But Jimmy never drives.

Napiao hold his hand up pretty soft. My friend says that good story, Jimmy and his car. These ones don't know Jimmy.

Okay, I says. Tell about Billy Frank and the dead-river pig. Funny story, that one, Billy Frank and the dead-river pig. Pretty big pig. Billy is real small, like Napiao, my friend. Hurt his back. Lost his truck.

Those ones like old stories, says my friend, maybe how the world was put together. Good Indian story like that, Napiao says. Those ones have tape recorders, he says.

Okay, I says.

Have some tea.

Stay awake.

Once upon a time.

Those stories start like that, pretty much, those ones, start on time. Anyway. There was nothing. Pretty hard to believe that, maybe.

You fellows keep listening, I says. Watch the floor. Be careful.

No water, no land, no stars, no moon. None of those things. Must have a sun someplace. Maybe not. Can't say. No Indians are there once upon a time. Lots of air. Only one person walk around. Call him god.

So.

They look around, and there is nothing. No grass. No fish. No trees. No mountains. No Indians, like I says. No white-man, either. Those come later, maybe one hundred years. Maybe not. That one god walk around, but pretty soon they get tired. Maybe that one says, we will get some stars. So he does. And then he says, maybe we should get a moon. So, they get one of them, too.

Someone write all this down, I don't know. Lots of things left to get.

Me-a-loo, call her deer.

Pa-pe-po, call her elk.

Tsling-ta, call her Blue-flower-berry.

Ga-ling, call her moon.

So-see-ka, call her flint.

A-ma-po, call her dog.

Ba-ko-zao, call her grocery store.

Pe-to-pa-zasling, call her television.

Pretty long list of things to get, that. Too many, maybe those ones say, how many more that one needs for world. So. Pretty soon that one can fix up real nice place. Not too hot. Not too cold. Like here, we sit here. My summer place is like that one.

I call my summer place O-say-ta-he-to-peo-teh. Means cool sleeping place. Other place, they call her Evening's garden. Good time to fish, that. Evening. Cool, not so hot. That Evening's garden like here.

Two human beings that one puts there. Call the man Ah-damn. Call the woman, Evening. Same as garden.

Okay.

She looks around her garden. Pretty nice place, that one. Good tree. Good deer. Good rock. Good water. Good sky. Good wind. No grocery store, no television.

Ah-damn and Evening real happy, those ones. No clothes, those, you know. Ha, Ha, Ha, Ha. But they pretty dumb, then. New, you know.

Have some tea.

Stay awake.

Good part is soon here.

That woman, Evening, she is curious, nosy, that one. She walk around the garden and she look everywhere. Look under rock. Look in grass. Look in sky. Look in water. Look in tree. So.

She find that tree, big one. Not like now, that tree. This one have lots of good things to eat. Have potato. Have pumpkin. Have corn. Have berries, all kind. Too many to say now.

This good tree also have some mee-so. Whiteman call them apples. This first woman look at the tree with the good things and she gets hungry. Make a meal in her head.

Leave that mee-so alone. Someone says that. Leave that mee-so alone. Leave that tree alone. The voice says that. Go away someplace else to eat!

That one, god. Hello, he's back.

Hey, says Evening, this is my garden.

You watch out, says that one, pretty loud voice. Sort of shout. Bad temper, that one. Maybe like Harley James. Bad temper, that one. Always shouting. Always with pulled-down mean look. Sometimes Harley come to town, drives his truck to town. Gets drunk. Drives back to that house. That one goes to town, get drunk, come home, that one, beat his wife. His wife leave. Goes back up north. Pretty mean one, that one. You boys know Harley James? Nobody there to beat up, now. Likes to shout, that one. Maybe you want to hear about Billy Frank and the dead-river pig?

Boy, my friend says, I can taste those mee-so. These boys pretty excited about those mee-so, I think.

Okay, I says.

Keep your eyes open, look around.

Evening, that one says, look pretty good, these. So she eat one, that mee-so. Boy, not bad, real juicy, that one. She is generous, Evening, good woman, that one. Brings mee-so to Ah-damn. I think he is busy then, writing things down. All the animals' names he writes somewhere, I don't know. Pretty boring that.

Deer come by, says Me-a-loo.

Elk come by, says Pa-pe-o.

Blue-flower-berry come by, says Tsling-ta.

Ah-damn not so smart like Evening, that one thinks Blue-flower-berry is animal, maybe.

Dog come by, says A-ma-po.

Raven come by, says Ne-co-tah.

Coyote come by, says Klee-qua.

Snail come by, says E-too.

Squirrel come by, says Qay-tha.

Owl come by, says Ba-tee-po-tah.

Weasel come by, says So-tha-nee-so.

Rabbit come by, says Klaaa-coo.

Flint come by, says So-see-ka.

Fish come by, says Laa-po.

Crayfish come by, says Tling.

Beaver come by, says Khan-yah-da.

Boy, all worn out. All those animals come by. Coyote come by maybe four, maybe eight times. Gets dressed up, fool around.

Says Piisto-pa.

Says Ho-ta-go.

Says Woho-i-kee.

Says Caw-ho-ha.

Ha, ha, ha, ha.

Tricky one, that coyote. Walks in circles. Sneaky.

That Ah-damn not so smart. Like Harley James, whiteman, those. Evening, she be Indian woman, I guess.

Evening come back. Hey, she says, what are all these coyote tracks come around in a circle. Not so smart, Ah-damn, pretty hungry though. Here, says Evening, mee-so, real juicy. So they do. Ah-damn, that one eat three mee-so. Ah-damn, says Evening, I better get some more mee-so.

Pretty soon that one, god, come by. He is pretty mad. You ate my mee-so, he says.

Don't be upset, says Evening, that one, first woman. Many more mee-so back there. Calm down, watch some television, she says.

But they are upset and that one says that Evening and Ah-damn better leave that good place, garden, Evening's garden, go somewhere else. Just like Indian today.

Evening says, okay, many good places around here. Ah-damn, that one wants to stay. But that fellow, god, whiteman I think, he says, you go too, you ate those mee-so, my mee-so.

Ah-damn is unhappy. He cry three times, ho, ho, ho. I only ate one, he says.

No, says that god fellow. I see everything. I see you eat three of my mee-so.

I only ate two, says Ah-damn but pretty quick that one throw him out.

Ha!

Throw him out on his back, right on those rocks. Ouch, ouch, ouch, that one says. Evening, she have to come back and fix him up before he is any good again. Alright.

There is also a Ju-poo-pea, whiteman call him snake. Don't

know what kind. Big white one maybe, I hear, maybe black, something else. I forgot this part. He lives in tree with mee-so. That one try to get friendly with Evening so she stick a mee-so in his mouth, that one. Crawl back into tree. Have trouble talking, hissss, hissss, hissss, hissss. Maybe he is still there. Like that dead-river pig and Billy Frank lose his truck.

So.

Evening and Ah-damn leave. Everybody else leave, too. That tree leave, too. Just god and Ju-poo-pea together.

Ah-damn and Evening come out here. Have a bunch of kids.

So.

That's all. It is ended.

Boy, my friend says, better get some more tea. One good story, that one, my friend, Napiao says.

Those men push their tape recorders, fix their cameras. All of those ones smile. Nod their head around. Look out window. Shake my hand. Make happy noises. Say goodbyes, see you later. Leave pretty quick.

We watch them go. My friend, Napiao, put the pot on for some tea. I clean up all the coyote tracks on the floor.

Totem

Beebe Hill stood at the reception desk of the Southwest Alberta Art Gallery and Prairie Museum and drummed her fingers on the counter until Walter Hooton came out of the director's office. She was annoyed, she told Walter, and she thought other people were annoyed, too, but were too polite to complain about the noises the totem pole in the far corner of the room was making.

"It sounds like gargling."

Walter assured her that there wasn't a totem pole in the entire place including the basement and the storage room. The current show, he explained, featured contemporary Canadian art from the Atlantic provinces.

"It's called 'Seaviews,'" Walter said, smiling with all his teeth showing. There had been, he admitted, a show on Northwest Coast carving at the gallery some nine years back, and, as he recalled, there might have been a totem pole in that exhibit.

Mrs. Hill, who was fifty-eight and quite used to men who smiled with all their teeth showing, took his hand and walked him to the back of the gallery. "Gargling," said Beebe. "It sounds like gargling."

Mrs. Hill and Mr. Hooton stood and looked at the corner for a very long time. "Well," said the director finally, "it certainly *looks* like a totem pole. But it doesn't sound at all like gargling. It sounds more like chuckling."

Mrs. Hill snorted and tossed her head over her shoulder. And what, she wanted to know, would a totem pole have to chuckle about. "In any case," said Mrs. Hill, "it is quite annoying, and I think the museum should do something about the problem." It would be a fine world, she pointed out, if paintings or photographs or abstract sculptures began carrying on like that.

Walter Hooton spent much of the afternoon going over the museum's records in an attempt to find out who owned the totem pole or where it had come from. At four o'clock, he gave up and called Larue Denny in the storeroom and asked him to grab Jimmy and a hand cart and meet him in the gallery.

"The problem," Walter explained to the two men, "is that this totem pole is not part of the show, and we need to move it someplace else."

"Where do you want us to take it," Larue wanted to know. "Storeroom is full."

"Find some temporary place, I suppose. I'm sure it's all a mistake, and when the secretary comes back on Monday, we'll have the whole thing straightened out."

"What's that sound?" asked Larue.

"We're not sure," said the director.

"Kinda loud," said Jimmy.

"Yes, it was bothering some of the patrons."

"Sort of like laughing," said Larue. "What do you think, Jimmy?"

Jimmy put his ear against the totem pole and listened. "It's sort of like a chant. Maybe it's Druidic."

"Druidic!"

"There was this movie about Druids on a flight from England to New York ... they did a lot of chanting ... the Druids ..."

Larue told Jimmy to tip the totem pole back so they could get the dolly under the base. But the totem pole didn't move. "Hey," he said, "it's stuck."

Larue pushed on the front, and Jimmy pulled on the top, and nothing happened. "It's really stuck."

Walter got on his hands and knees and looked at the bottom. Then he took his glasses out of their case and put them on. "It appears," he said, "that it goes right through the floor."

Both Larue and Jimmy got down with the director. Larue shook his head. "It doesn't make any sense," he said, "because the floor's concrete. I was here when they built this building, and I don't remember them pouring the floor around a totem pole."

"We could get the chainsaw and cut it off close to the floor," Jimmy volunteered.

"Well, we can't have it making noises in the middle of a show on seascapes," said Walter. "Do what you have to do, but do it quietly."

After the gallery closed for the evening, Larue and Jimmy took the chainsaw out of its case and put on their safety goggles. Larue held the totem pole and Jimmy cut through the base, the chain screaming, the wood chips flying all around the gallery. Some of the larger chips bounced off the paintings and left small dents in the swirling waves and the glistening rocks and the seabirds floating on the wind. Then they loaded the totem pole on a dolly and put it in the basement near the boiler.

"Listen to that," said Jimmy, knocking the sawdust off his pants. "It's still making that noise."

When Walter arrived at the gallery on Monday morning, the secretary was waiting for him. "We have a problem, Mr. Hooton," she said. "There is a totem pole in the corner, and it's grunting."

"Damn!" said Hooton, and he called Larue and Jimmy.

"You're right," said Larue, after he and Jimmy had looked at the totem pole. "It does sound like grunting. Doesn't sound a thing like the other one. What do you want us to do with this one?"

"Get rid of it," said Walter. "And watch the paintings this time."

Larue and Jimmy got the chainsaw and the safety goggles and the dolly, and moved the totem pole into the basement alongside the first one.

"That wasn't hard," said the director.

"Those grunts were pretty disgusting," said the secretary.

"Yes, they were," agreed Walter.

After lunch, the totem pole in the corner of the gallery started shouting, loud, explosive shouts that echoed through the collection of sea scenes and made the paintings on the wall tremble ever so slightly. When Walter returned, the secretary was sitting at her desk with her hands over her ears.

"My God!" said Walter. "How did this happen?"

That evening, Walter and Larue and Jimmy sat in Walter's

office and talked about the problem. "The trick I think," said Larue, "is to cut the pole down and then cover the stump with pruning paste. That way it won't grow back."

"What about the shouting?"

"Well, you can't hear it much from the basement."

"Alright," said Walter. "We'll give that a try. How many poles are in storage?"

"Three with this one, and we haven't got room for any more."

The next day, the totem pole in the corner was singing. It started with a high, wailing, nasal sound and then fell back into a patient, rhythmic drone that gave Walter a huge headache just above his eyes and made him sweat.

"This is getting to be a real problem," he told Larue and Jimmy. "If we can't solve it, we may have to get some government assistance."

"Provincial?"

"It could be more serious than that," said Walter.

"Maybe we should just leave it," said Jimmy.

"We can't just leave it there," said the director. "We need the space for our other shows, and we can't have it singing all the time, either."

"Maybe if we ignore it, it will stop singing," said Jimmy. "It might even go away or disappear or something. Besides, we don't have any place to put it. Maybe, after a while, you wouldn't even notice it ... like living next to the train tracks or by a highway."

"Sure," said Larue, who was tired of cutting down totem poles and trying to find space for them. "Couldn't hurt to give that a try."

The totem pole stayed in the corner, but Jimmy and Larue

were right. After the first week, the singing didn't bother Walter nearly as much, and, by the end of the month, he hardly noticed it at all.

Nonetheless, Walter remained mildly annoyed that the totem pole continued to take up space and inexplicably irritated by the low, measured pulse that rose out of the basement and settled like fine dust on the floor.

Magpies

This one is about Granny. Reserve story. Everyone knows this story. Wilma knows it. Ambrose knows it. My friend, Napioa. Lionel James.. Billy Frank knows it, too. Billy Frank hears this story in Calgary. He hears it three times. Maybe six. Boy, he tells me, here comes that story again.

Sometimes this story is about Wilma. Some people tell it so Ambrose is all over the place. The way I tell it is this way and I tell it this way all the time.

Sometimes I tell you about those Magpies first. With those noses. Good noses, those ones. Magpies talk all the time, you know. Good gossips, those. Hahahahaha. Good jokes, too. Sometimes I start that way.

Okay. Here comes that story again.

Granny falls and hurts her leg. So, that leg is pink. Then it looks blue. Another time it is black. Yellow for a long time. That leg. Granny's leg.

Granny looks at that leg and thinks about dying. So she talks about falling over dead. When that Granny starts talking about being dead, Wilma says no, no, no. That is just a bruise. Yellow bruise. Those ones are okay.

Granny talks to everyone she see about dying. I'm going to die, she says to me and I say yes, that's right. Old people know these things. It happens. Maybe that blood thing. Maybe cigarettes. Maybe a truck. Maybe that bottle. Granny likes to talk of dying. I'm going to be dead real soon, she says. Going to rot and nobody comes by but those birds tell all those stories and laugh.

Watch those Magpies, that old woman tells Ambrose. You see them?

Sure, says Ambrose.

They smell death, she says. Isn't that right?

Yes, I says, that's true.

Those ones take the eyes first, she says, soft parts. Nice round parts they like first. Ripe. That's why you got to wrap them tight.

That's right, I says.

You listening Ambrose? That old Granny shake Ambrose so he is awake. They smell death, those birds, like you smell chokecherries on the boil. When I die, they'll come to me like that.

You can count on me, says Ambrose.

I'm going to die, then, Granny tells me, and I says okay.

Wilma takes that old woman to the hospital to see two, maybe five white doctors. They look at the leg. They look at that leg again. They do it some more times, too. Ummmm, ummmm, ummmm. That way. In the mouth. They don't dance. They don't sing. They think they talking to Granny. Ummmm, ummmm, ummmm.

Granny says to me there are good places to die. River is a

good one. Coulees is okay, too. Maybe a mountain. Bad places, too, she says. Grocery store. Shopping mall. Movie show. Hospital.

That hospital is one bad place to die. See-po-aah-loo. See-po-aah-loo is like a hole. In the ground. See-po-aah-loo is one old word. Where you put stew bones. Where you put old things that are broke. Where you put old things that smell bad. Where you put beer cans. Coffee grounds. Fish guts. Milk cartons. Newspapers. Tractor oil. That black dog Walter Turnbull hit with his truck. Everything you don't want people to see. You put them there. See-po-aah-loo.

Then you cover it up. Go someplace else.

Hospital.

Those doctors tell Granny, ummmm, ummmm, ummmm. Maybe you better stay here. One day. Four days. Maybe we see something. Ummmm, ummmm, ummmm. Ambrose says Whites go to that hospital to get a new nose. Get good breasts. Fix up that old butt. Haul out things you don't need no more. Ambrose tells me that. Fix you up. Like a car. Run better. Ummmm, ummmm, ummmm.

Those ones don't fool Granny. I can tell you that.

That Granny nod her head. Look at that floor. Look at that door. Shuffle her feet. Like a Round dance. Ho-ho-ho-ho, that one dances out of See-po-aah-loo. Don't want to be in no hole, she says.

God loves you, Granny, Wilma says. Good woman, that Wilma. Loves Granny. Fixes her food. Washes her clothes. Wilma is mostly Catholic in the middle. Knows about dying. Reads those papers you get from church. In that wood pocket. Near that water.

When God takes you, Momma, you'll be real happy. This is

how Wilma talks. Dead is okay, Wilma says. That God fellow just waiting for you. Good to see you. Howdy-do.

Don't put me in that grave, See-po-aah-loo, Granny tell Wilma.

Garbage hole.

Hospital.

One word. You see?

Yes, says Wilma, that's the modern way. You need a priest. He can make it clean.

Holes are cold, Granny says.

God will keep you warm, Wilma says.

So, Granny finds Ambrose.

Ambrose is a big man. Big chest. Big legs. Big head. Friendly man that Ambrose. Have a joke. Have a story. Always thinking about things to do. Going to fix this thing. Going to fix that thing. Granny finds Ambrose. You fix this thing for me, she says. Yes, that one says, I will do it. You can count on me.

Granny brings that boy to my house. Ho, I says, you got your big boy with you. Yes, she says, we come to see you, talk with you. Sit down, I says. Coffee is here. Tea, too. Sit down and eat some food.

You must talk to my big boy, Granny says. Tell him the way. Show him how to do this thing. You listen to this old one, Granny says. You can count on me, Ambrose says.

Granny squeeze her eyes. You be here when I die. You tell Wilma how to do this thing. You look out for me, take care of me, my big boy.

You can count on me.

I'm counting on you, says Granny. In that cottonwood at Heavyshield's cabin. Aoo-lee-sth. That's the one. Other ways that hole will get me and I'll come back.

You can count on me.

That leg get better. Granny's leg. But Granny dies anyway. Later. Not right now. Two, maybe four years. Maybe more. She falls over dead then. Like that. It is finished.

Ambrose is not there when Granny dies. Someone says he is in Edmonton at those meetings. Someone says, no, he is in Toronto. Someone says he is across the line. Wilma sniff her nose this way and that one sniff her nose that way. We can't wait for that Ambrose maybe come along. We going to do this thing right, Wilma says. We going to do this thing now.

So they get a priest.

So they put Granny in a box.

So they stick Granny in the church.

So they throw her in a hole.

Just like that. Pretty quick. They put her in that hole before Ambrose comes home. Everyone stands there. Ho ho ho ho. All of them feel bad, Granny in that hole. Wilma cries, too. Smack her hands and says, that's okay now. Everything is done now. It is finished.

Aoh-quwee.

That's the end of the story.

No, I was just fooling.

There's more.

Stick around.

Okay. Ambrose comes home. Everyone figures out this part, Ambrose comes home. No smile. No happy joke. Momma is with God, Wilma says. She's happy. Nothing for you to do.

I gave her this promise, Ambrose says, and I says, yes, that's right.

Keep your promise in your pocket, Wilma says. Momma don't need that promise. Everything is pretty good. God's got her.

God don't live in a hole, says Ambrose.

God is everywhere, says Wilma.

Those two talk like that. One day, maybe two, three weeks. Talk about God. Talk about that promise. You make lots of promises, Wilma says. Those things are easy for you to make. They fall out of your mouth like spit. Everybody got three or four of them.

That part is true. I can tell you that. Ambrose is generous with those things. Those promises. I help you chop wood for winter, Ambrose tells my friend Napioa. Fix that truck for you, he says to Billy Frank. Going to dig that ditch tomorrow, he tells his uncle.

You can count on me.

Keep that promise in your pocket, Wilma tells that one.

Ambrose comes to my house. Ho, he says, we got to fix that window. Yes, I says, it is broke alright. Maybe I'll bring some tools out next week, he says. Yes, I says, that would be good.

That Ambrose sits down and starts to cry. Hoo hoo hoo hoo. Like that. That big boy cries like that. Sit down, I says. Have some tea.

You got to help me, he says. Sure, I says. I can do that.

Granny's in that hole, he says. She's going to come back. You got to help me do this thing. We got to get her out and do it right. Put her in that tree. Heavyshield's tree. In the mountains. Like she said.

Boy, I says, lots of work that. They put her in pretty deep. Way down there. With that God fellow.

I can dig her up, Ambrose says. You don't have to do

anything. I'll dig her up and get you and you can tell me how to do this thing. Got to keep that promise.

Okay, I says.

So.

That Ambrose gets everything we need. Wilma watches him and sniffs with her nose. Tonight I'm going to do it, Ambrose says. But he doesn't. Flat tire, he says.

Tonight I'm going to do it, that one tells me. But he doesn't. No moon.

Tonight I'm going to do it. That big boy has one good memory. But he doesn't do it then, either. Got the flu.

Ambrose gets a skin and he keeps that skin in the back of his truck. Green. Getting to smell, I think. Maybe not. Those Magpies hang around that truck. What you got in that truck, Wilma says. Nothing, says Ambrose. Just some stuff.

But you know, he does it. That big boy comes to my house early in the morning. With his truck. With that skin. With Granny sewed up in that skin. Just like I said. Ho, I says, you got that Granny. Yes, says Ambrose, I dig her up last night. Now we can do it right.

So we do. Ambrose drives that truck with Granny sewed up in the skin to Heavyshield's cabin and that good boy climbs that tree and that one drags Granny up that tree with a rope. High. On those skinny branches. Near the sun. He puts that old woman. Then he climbs down. There, he says, and smacks his hands together. That does it.

I make some tea. Ambrose sits on the ground, watches Granny in the tree. Pretty soon he is asleep.

Let's see what happens.

Well, pretty quick those Magpies come along and look in that tree. And they fly in that tree. And they sit in that tree.

Talking. They sit on that hide has Granny hid inside and talk to her. Hello. Nice day.

Then that sun comes down. Into the tree. With those birds. With Granny. Ho, that sun says, what we got here? Granny and a bunch of Magpies. That's right, I says.

Then that big dust ball comes along, right up to the house. Heavyshield's place. Rolls into the yard.

Then Wilma gets out.

Then the RCMP gets out.

Then Benny Goodrunner, tribal policeman, gets out.

Out of that dust ball.

Boy, those birds are some fast talkers.

Where's Granny, Wilma says. Where's Ambrose? She says that, too. Where's Ambrose Standing Bull, RCMP says. Benny don't say nothing. He just stand there. Look embarrassed.

Ambrose wakes up. Wilma sees him wake up. There he is, she says. There is that criminal. There is that thief. Then she uses words I don't understand.

Ambrose stands right up. I'm just doing what Granny asked. Nothing wrong with that.

That RCMP got his bright uniform on. Body-stealing is against the law, he says.

This is reserve land, Ambrose says.

Benny's going to arrest you, Ambrose, says Wilma. Going to put you in jail for digging up Granny.

Lots of Magpies in the tree now. They just listening. All ears.

Wilma looks in that tree. She sees those birds. She sees that sun. She sees that hide. He's already stuck her in that tree. We got to bring her down.

RCMP man looks at Wilma and looks at Benny. Wilma looks at Benny. Ambrose looks at Benny. Maybe you boys want some tea, I says. Nice evening. Maybe you want to sit and have some tea.

No time for tea, old one, Wilma says in our language. My mother's in that tree. We got to get her down.

So. Benny is the one. Have to climb that tree. All the way. So, he starts up. Those birds stop walking on Granny and watch Benny. Ambrose watches Benny. Wilma watches Benny. RCMP man watches Benny. That Benny is a rodeo man, rides those bulls. Strong legs, that one. He climbs all the way to Granny. Then he sits down. On a limb. Like those birds. Hey, he says, I can see the river. Real good view.

Look for Granny, says that Wilma.

Leave her alone, says Ambrose.

Boy, those Magpies are jumping around in that tree. Dancing. Choosing sides. Singing songs. Telling jokes.

Milk carton comes out of that tree.

Peach can comes out of that tree.

Bottle of Wesson cooking oil comes down. Empty.

Carburetor.

Magazine.

Hey, says Benny. Granny's not here. She's not in this skin. She's gone. Nothing here but garbage. Benny comes down that tree.

Everybody looks at Ambrose.

Must be magic, says Ambrose and he walks into that cabin and closes the door.

Wilma stands up straight and she looks at that RCMP man. Benny has his clothes all dirty. That RCMP is mostly clean. Nothing but garbage in that tree, Benny says. Alright, says Wilma. She gets back in the truck, that one. Benny gets in that truck. RCMP gets in that truck.

Boy, pretty exciting.

That sun gets down behind the mountain. Ambrose comes out of that house, says, everybody gone? Yes, I says. Good trick, that one, he says. Yes, I says, that one had me fooled. My shovel broke, says Ambrose. I'm going to get her tonight. Nobody will see me this time. I would have got her that other time but my shovel broke. You got a shovel I can borrow? Sure, I say, you can use my good shovel.

You watch, says Ambrose. This is my plan. Benny saw that bag of garbage. So now I get Granny and put her up there. Take that garbage down and put Granny in that tree like I promise. No one will look there again. That's my plan.

That's a good plan, I says. That should fool them. Good thing you got some of that garbage out of the ground.

You got to promise me you won't tell anyone about my plan, Ambrose says. Watch out for those birds, I says. They told Wilma about your bag of garbage, I bet. They got good ears, those ones. You got to sing that song so they can't hear. So they won't remember. You know that song?

No, say Ambrose. You better listen then, I says. Otherwise those birds will tell everyone what your plan is. So I show Ambrose the song and he sings it pretty good, that boy. And he borrows my shovel. My good shovel. And I don't see him for a long time. And I don't see Wilma either. And I don't tell Ambrose's plan.

But I know what happened.

But I can't tell.

I promised.

You can count on me.

Trap
Lines

When I was twelve, thirteen at the most, and we were still living on the reserve, I asked my grandmother and she told me my father sat in the bathroom in the dark because it was the only place he could go to get away from us kids. What does he do in the bathroom, I wanted to know. Sits, said my grandmother. That's it? Thinks, she said, he thinks. I asked her if he went to the bathroom, too, and she said that was adult conversation, and I would have to ask him. It seemed strange at the time, my father sitting in the dark, thinking, but rather than run the risk of asking him, I was willing to believe my grandmother's explanation.

At forty-six, I am sure it was true, though I have had some trouble convincing my son that sitting in the bathroom with the lights out is normal. He has, at eighteen, come upon language, much as a puppy comes upon a slipper. Unlike other teenagers his age who slouch in closets and basements, mute and desolate, Christopher likes to chew on conversation, toss it in the air, bang it off the walls. I was always shy around language. Christopher is fearless.

"Why do you sit in the bathroom, Dad?"

"My father used to sit in the bathroom."

"How many bathrooms did you have in the olden days?"

"We lived on the reserve then. We only had the one."

"I thought you guys lived in a teepee or something. Where was the bathroom?"

"That was your great grandfather. We lived in a house."

"It's a good thing we got two bathrooms," he told me.

The house on the reserve had been a government house, small and poorly made. When we left and came to the city, my father took a picture of it with me and my sisters standing in front. I have the picture in a box somewhere. I want to show it to Christopher, so he can see just how small the house was.

"You're always bragging about that shack."

"It wasn't a shack."

"The one with all the broken windows?"

"Some of them had cracks."

"And it was cold, right?"

"In the winter it was cold."

"And you didn't have television."

"That's right."

"Jerry says that every house built has cable built in. It's a law or something."

"We didn't have cable or television."

"Is that why you left?"

"My father got a job here. I've got a picture of the house. You want to see it?"

"No big deal."

"I can probably find it."

"No big deal."

Some of these conversations were easy. Others were hard.

My conversations with my father were generally about the weather or trapping or about fishing. That was it.

"Jerry says his father has to sit in the bathroom, too."

"Shower curtain was bundled up again. You have to spread it out so it can dry."

"You want to know why?"

"Be nice if you cleaned up the water you leave on the floor."

"Jerry says it's because his father's constipated."

"Lawn has to be mowed. It's getting high."

"He says it's because his father eats too much junk food."

"Be nice if you cleaned the bottom of the mower this time. It's packed with grass."

"But that doesn't make any sense, does it? Jerry and I eat junk food all the time, and we're not constipated."

"Your mother wants me to fix the railing on the porch. I'm going to need your help with that."

"Are you constipated?"

Alberta wasn't much help. I could see her smiling to herself whenever Christopher started chewing. "It's because we're in the city," she said. "If we had stayed on the reserve, Christopher would be out on a trap line with his mouth shut and you wouldn't be constipated."

"Nobody runs a trap line anymore."

"My grandfather said the outdoors was good for you."

"We could have lived on the reserve, but you didn't want to."

"And he was never constipated."

"My father ran a trap line. We didn't leave the reserve until I was sixteen. Your folks have always lived in the city."

"Your father was a mechanic."

"He ran a trap line, just like his father."

"Your grandfather was a mechanic."

"Not in the winter."

My father never remarried. After my mother died, he just looked after the four of us. He seldom talked about himself, and, slowly, as my sisters and I got older, he became a mystery. He remained a mystery until his death.

"You hardly even knew my father," I said. "He died two years after we were married."

Alberta nodded her head and stroked her hair behind her ears. "Your grandmother told me."

"She died before he did."

"My mother told me. She knew your grandmother."

"So, what did your mother tell you?"

"She told me not to marry you."

"She told me I was a damn good catch. Those were her exact words, 'damn good.'"

"She said that just to please you. She said you had a smart mouth. She wanted me to marry Sid."

"So, why didn't you marry Sid?"

"I didn't love Sid."

"What else did she say?"

"She said that constipation ran in your family."

After Christopher graduated from high school, he pulled up in front of the television and sat there for almost a month.

"You planning on going to university?" I asked him.

"I guess."

"You going to do it right away or you going to get a job?"

"I'm going to rest first."

"Seems to me, you got to make some decisions."

"Maybe I'll go in the bathroom later on and think about it."

"You can't just watch television."

"I know."

"You're an adult now."

"I know."

Alberta called these conversations father and son talks, and you could tell the way she sharpened her tongue on "father and son" that she didn't think much of them.

"You ever talk to him about important things?"

"Like what?"

"You know."

"Sure."

"Okay, what do you tell him?"

"I tell him what he needs to know."

"My mother talked to my sisters and me all the time. About everything."

"We have good conversations."

"Did he tell you he isn't going to college."

"He just wants some time to think."

"Not what he told me."

I was in a bookstore looking for the new Audrey Thomas novel. The Ts were on the third shelf down and I had to bend over and cock my head to one side in order to read the titles. As I stood there, bent over and twisted, I felt my face start to slide. It was a strange sensation. Everything that wasn't anchored to bone just slipped off the top half of my head, slopped into the lower half, and hung there like a bag of jello. When I arrived home, I got myself into the same position in front of the bathroom mirror. That evening, I went downstairs and sat on the couch with Christopher and waited for a commercial.

"How about turning off the sound?"

"We going to have another talk?"

"I thought we could talk about the things that you're good at doing."

"I'm not good at anything."

"That's not true. You're good at computers."

"I like the games."

"You're good at talking to people. You could be a teacher."

"Teaching looks boring. Most of my teachers were boring."

"Times are tougher now," I said. "When your grandfather was a boy, he worked on a trap line up north. It was hard work, but you didn't need a university degree. Now you have to have one. Times are tougher."

"Mr. Johnson was the boringest of all."

"University is the key. Lot of kids go there not knowing what they want to do, and, after two or three years, they figure it out. Have you applied to any universities yet?"

"Commercial's over."

"No money in watching television."

"Commercial's over."

Alberta caught me bent over in front of the mirror. "You lose something?"

"Mirror's got a defect in it. You can see it just there."

"At least you're not going bald."

"I talked to Christopher about university."

"My father never looked a day over forty." Alberta grinned at herself in the mirror so she could see her teeth. "You know," she said, "When you stand like that, your face hangs funny."

I don't remember my father growing old. He was fifty-six when he died. We never had long talks about life or careers. When I was a kid—I forget how old—we drove into Medicine

River to watch the astronauts land on the moon. We sat in the American Hotel and watched it on the old black and white that Morris Rough Dog kept in the lobby. Morris told my father that they were checking the moon to see if it had any timber, water, valuable minerals, or game, and, if it didn't, they planned to turn it into a reserve and move all the Cree up there. Hey, he said to my father, what's that boy of yours going to be when he grows up? Beats me, said my father. Well, said Morris, there's damn little money in the hotel business and sure as hell nothing but scratch and splinters in being an Indian.

For weeks after, my father told Morris's story about the moon and the astronauts. My father laughed when he told the story. Morris had told it straight-faced.

"What do you really do in the bathroom, Dad?"

"I think."

"That all?"

"Just thinking."

"Didn't know thinking smelled so bad."

My father liked the idea of fishing. There were always fishing magazines around the house, and he would call me and my sisters over to show us a picture of a rainbow trout breaking water, or a northern pike rolled on its side or a tarpon sailing out of the blue sea like a silver missile. At the back of the magazines were advertisements for fishing tackle that my father would cut out and stick on the refrigerator door. When they got yellow and curled up, he would take them down and put up fresh ones.

I was in the downstairs bathroom. Christopher and Jerry were in Christopher's room. I could hear them playing video games and talking.

"My father wants me to go into business with him," said Jerry.

"Yeah."

"Can you see it? Me, selling cars the rest of my life?"

"Good money?"

"Sure, but what a toady job. I'd rather go to university and see what comes up."

"I'm thinking about that, too."

"What's your dad want you to do," said Jerry.

It was dark in the bathroom and cool, and I sat there trying not to breathe.

"Take a guess."

"Doctor?" said Jerry. "Lawyer?"

"Nope."

"An accountant? My dad almost became an accountant."

"You'll never guess. You could live to be a million years old and you'd never guess."

"Sounds stupid."

"A trapper. He wants me to work a trap line."

"You got to be kidding."

"God's truth. Just like my grandfather."

"Your dad is really weird."

"You ought to live with him."

We only went fishing once. It was just before my mother died. We all got in the car and drove up to a lake just off the reserve. My dad rented a boat and took us kids out in pairs. My mother stayed on the docks and lay in the sun.

Towards the end of the day, my sisters stayed on the dock with my mother, and my father and I went out in the boat alone. He had a new green tackle box he had bought at the hardware store on Saturday. Inside was an assortment of hooks and spinners and lures and a couple of red things with long trailing red and white skirts. He snorted and showed me a clipping that had come with the box for a lure that could actually call the fish.

Used to be beaver all around here, he told me, but they've been trapped out. Do you know why the beavers were so easy to catch, he asked me. It's because they always do the same thing. You can count on beavers to be regular. They're not stupid. They're just predictable, so you always set the trap in the same place and you always use the same bait, and pretty soon, they're gone.

Trapping was good money when your grandfather was here, but not now. No money in being a mechanic either. Better think of something else to do. Maybe I'll be an astronaut, I said. Have more luck trying to get pregnant, he said. Maybe I'll be a fisherman. No sir, he said. All the money's in making junk like this, and he squeezed the advertisement into a ball and set it afloat on the lake.

Christopher was in front of the television when I got home from work on Friday. There was a dirty plate under the coffee table and a box of crackers sitting on the cushions.

"What do you say we get out of the house this weekend and do something?"

"Like what?"

"I don't know. What would you like to do?"

"We could go to that new movie."

"I meant outdoors."

"What's to do outdoors besides work?"

"We could go fishing."

"Fishing?"

"Sure, I used to go fishing with my father all the time."

"This one of those father, son things?"

"We could go to the lake and rent a boat."

"I may have a job."

"Great. Where?"

"Let you know later."

"What's the secret?"

"No secret. I'll just tell you later."

"What about the fishing trip?"

"Better stick around the house in case someone calls."

Christopher slumped back into the cushions and turned up the sound on the television.

"What about the dirty plate?"

"It's not going anywhere."

"That box is going to spill if you leave it like that."

"It's empty."

My father caught four fish that day. I caught two. He sat in the stern with the motor. I sat in the bow with the anchor. When the sun dropped into the trees, he closed his tackle box and gave the starter rope a pull. The motor sputtered and died. He pulled it again. Nothing. He moved his tackle box out of the way, stood up, and put one foot on the motor and gave the rope a hard yank. It broke in his hand and he tumbled over backwards, the boat tipping and slopping back and forth. Damn, he said, and he pulled himself back up on the seat. Well, son, he said, I've got a job for you, and he set the oars in the locks and leaned against the motor. He looked around the lake at the trees and the mountains and the sky. And he looked at me. Try not to get me wet, he said.

Alberta was in the kitchen peeling a piece of pizza away from the box. "Christopher got a job at that new fast food place. Did he tell you?"

"No. He doesn't tell me those things."

"You should talk with him more."

"I talk with him all the time."

"He needs to know you love him."

"He knows that."

"He just wants to be like you."

Once when my sister and I were fighting, my father broke us up and sent us out in the woods to get four sticks apiece about as round as a finger. So we did. And when we brought them back, he took each one and broke it over his knee. Then he sent us out to get some more.

"Why don't you take him fishing?"

"I tried. He didn't want to go."

"What did you and your father do?"

"We didn't do much of anything."

"Okay, start there."

When we came home with the sticks, my father wrapped them all together with some cord. Try to break these, he said. We jumped on the sticks and we kicked them. We put the bundle between two rocks and hit it with a board. But the sticks didn't break. Finally, my father took the sticks and tried to break them across his knee. You kids get the idea, he said. After my father went back into the house, my youngest sister kicked the sticks around the yard some more and said it was okay but she'd rather have a ball.

Christopher's job at the fast food place lasted three weeks. After that he resumed his place in front of the television.

"What happened with the job?"

"It was boring."

"Lots of jobs are boring."

"Don't worry, I'll get another."

"I'm not worried," I said, and I told him about the sticks. "A stick by itself is easy to break, but it's impossible to break them when they stand together. You see what I mean?"

"Chainsaw," said my son.

"What?"

"Use a chainsaw."

I began rowing for the docks, and my father began to sing. Then he stopped and leaned forward as though he wanted to tell me something. Son, he said, I've been thinking ... And just then a gust of wind blew his hat off, and I had to swing the boat around so we could get it before it sank. The hat was waterlogged. My father wrung it out as best he could, and then he settled in against the motor again and started singing.

My best memory of my father was that day on the lake. He lived alone, and, after his funeral, my sisters and I went back to his apartment and began packing and dividing the things as we went. I found his tackle box in the closet at the back.

"Christopher got accepted to university."

"When did that happen?"

"Last week. He said he was going to tell you."

"Good."

"He and Jerry both got accepted. Jerry's father gave Jerry a car and they're going to drive over to Vancouver and see about getting jobs before school starts."

"Vancouver, huh?"

"Not many more chances."

"What?"

"For talking to your son."

Jerry came by on a Saturday, and Alberta and I helped Christopher pack his things in the station wagon.

"Nice car," said Alberta.

"It's a pig," said Jerry. "My father couldn't sell it because of the color. But it'll get us there."

"Bet your father and mother are going to miss you."

"My father wanted me to stick around and help with the business. Gave me this big speech about traditions."

"Nothing wrong with traditions," Alberta said.

"Yeah, I guess. Look at this." Jerry held up a red metal tool box. "It's my grandfather's first tool box. My father gave it to me. You know, father to son and all that."

"That's nice," said Alberta.

"I guess."

"Come on," said Christopher. "Couple more things and we can get going."

Alberta put her arm around my waist and she began to poke me. Not so you could see. Just a sharp, annoying poke. "For Christ's sake," she whispered, "say something."

Christopher came out of the house carrying his boots and a green metal box. "All set," he said.

"Where'd you get the box?" I asked.

"It's an old fishing tackle box."

"I know."

"It's been sitting in the closet for years. Nobody uses it."

"It was my father's box."

"Yeah. It's got some really weird stuff in it. Jerry says that there's good fishing in B.C."

"That's right," said Jerry. "You should see some of those salmon."

"You don't fish."

"You never took me."

"My father gave me that box. It was his father's."

"You never use it."

"No, it's okay. I was going to give it to you anyway."

"No big deal. I can leave it here."

"No, it's yours."

"I'll take care of it."

"Maybe after you get settled out there, we can come out. Maybe you and I can do some fishing."

"Sure."

"Love you, honey," said Alberta and she put her arms around Christopher and held him. "I'm going to miss you. Call us if you need anything. And watch what you eat so you don't wind up like your father."

"Sure."

Alberta and I stood in the yard for a while after the boys drove off. "You could have told him you loved him," she said.

"I did. In my own way."

"Oh, he's supposed to figure that out because you gave him that old fishing box."

"That's the way my father did it."

"I thought you told me you found the box when you and your sisters were cleaning out his place."

After supper, Alberta went grocery shopping. I sat in the bathroom and imagined what my father had been going to say just before the wind took his hat, something important I guessed, something I could have shared with my son.

How
Corporal
Colin Sterling
Saved
Blossom, Alberta,
and Most of the
Rest of the World
as Well

The bright prairie sun was just above the tops of the trailers when Ralph Lawton's wife, Bella, rolled over and shook Ralph.

"Are you awake?"

Ralph grunted.

"Did you hear those damn Indians?"

"Coyotes," said Ralph.

"I know Indians when I hear them. Drinking, I suspect."

"Coyotes."

"Did they pay you in advance?"

"It was the coyotes you heard last night."

"Then they've flown the coop by now."

There was snow on the ground, and the air was cold. Ralph looked out of the window of the office. Room sixteen seemed quiet enough. He put on his robe.

"Dead drunk, the lot of them," Bella yelled from the bedroom.

"Coyotes," said Ralph quietly to himself.

Ralph walked down to room sixteen. The pick-up that the

Indians had arrived in was still parked in front of the room.

He knocked on the door. The knock was perfunctory. The pass key was already in his other hand.

"Maid service," said Ralph, and he opened the door and stepped inside.

Inside the RCMP detachment at Blossom, the air was heavy with the warm smell of fresh doughnuts and hot coffee. Corporal Colin Sterling sat behind the large oak desk. He rubbed the side of his nose, picked at a hair growing out of a brown mole near his ear, and considered the cardboard box on the desk in front of him. There were few things that Corporal Sterling liked better than the doughnuts that Bernie, over at the Chinook Café, made. He cleared his throat and reached out, helping himself to a large chocolate-covered cake doughnut.

"Mrs. Post," he said to the woman at the switchboard. "Would you care for a doughnut?"

Normally, Corporal Sterling would have had to compete for the doughnuts with Constable Takas and Constable Gromski, but both men had been called to the reserve.

"I went yesterday," Corporal Sterling had said. "It's your turn." Both Constable Takas and Constable Gromski grumbled a bit, but they put their jackets on. Constable Takas threw several of the glazed and jelly-centered doughnuts into an exhibit bag.

"Not too many, now," said Corporal Sterling, wagging a sugar-coated finger at Constable Takas. "Too much sugar is bad for you." Corporal Sterling leaned over and selected a glazed with a raspberry center.

Corporal Sterling was just finishing his eighth doughnut when Thelma Post turned in her chair. "It's Ralph over at the

Chief Mountain Motel," she said. "Says he's got a mass murder on his hands."

Corporal Sterling had been with the RCMP for sixteen years. The last four had been spent in Blossom. "Ask him if he's been drinking again."

"He says," said Thelma, "to get your 'you know what' over here."

Corporal Sterling pushed away from the desk and stood up. "Fiddle," he said and reached for a spice with white frosting.

Room sixteen at the Chief Mountain Motel was just like room twenty-two or room seven. They all had showers, two beds, a plug-in pot for tea, and a color television set. Room sixteen also had six bodies.

"Bunch of Indians came in last night," Ralph Lawton said, and he waved his hand around the room. "Told them not to bust the place up. Business has been pretty slow, you know. They paid cash. Just don't bust the place up. That's what I told them."

Corporal Sterling leaned over the first body, which was on the floor beside the bed.

"Bloody hell, Ralph," said Corporal Sterling. "These fellows aren't dead. They're still breathing. This one's singing."

Ralph took one of the Indians by a foot and shook him. "Oh yeah ... oh yeah?" said Ralph. "You ever see anyone this stiff who wasn't dead?" Ralph shook the man again. It was like wiggling a two-by-four. "You ever see anything like this?"

Corporal Sterling looked at the Indian and then leaned closer as if he were trying to hear what the man was saying. "That's odd," he said, and he stood up. Corporal Sterling rubbed the side of his nose and picked at the hair. "When I was stationed at the subdivision in Lethbridge," he began, "we

picked up a fellow behind the Alec Arms who was so drunk ...
well, he was ... 'stiff.'"

Ralph was not having a good time. "What are you, some
kind of asshole comic? No one gets this stiff from drinking."

"Let's not be overwrought," said Corporal Sterling.

The six Indians in room sixteen were lying in a neat row.
There was one on the floor, two on the first bed, a fourth on
the floor between the two beds, and two more on the second
bed. All of them were absolutely rigid.

"You can feel a pulse," said Corporal Sterling. "A tad slow,
though. I think he's stopped singing now, too. You'd better
call Doctor Phelps."

By the time Doctor Phelps arrived at the Chief Mountain
Motel in Blossom, Alberta, Thelma, at the detachment office,
had called to tell Corporal Sterling that Constable Takas and
Constable Gromski had phoned in with a problem.

"Look," said Thelma. "They told me to get a hold of you
right away. And all *I* know is what they told me. Rock-hard
Indians. That's exactly what they said. Thirty or forty Indians,
all as hard as rocks."

Doctor Phelps spent the better part of an hour examining
the Indians.

"They're alive alright," he said.

"We know that," said Ralph. "What the hell is wrong with
them?"

"Can't tell yet. I've seen them drunk, beat up, suicidal, half-
dead from drinking lighter fluid and vanilla extract. I've seen
them broke and I've seen them rolling in money. But this is
new."

"Could it be contagious?" said Corporal Sterling.

"Always the chance, I suppose."

"Then," said Corporal Sterling, wiggling his neck into his collar, "we shall have to quarantine the motel."

Ralph, who was not having a good time at all, said, "Oh yeah ... oh yeah ... just close the motel. As if business isn't slow enough. Half a dozen Indians go and get stiff on me and ... poof! ... I'm out of business."

"Did any of them say anything?" asked Doctor Phelps.

"Not a damn thing," said Ralph Lawton.

Corporal Sterling pulled at the hair near his ear. "As a matter of fact," he said, "the one chap was mumbling something. Sounded like he was singing at first."

"So," said Doctor Phelps, "what was he singing?"

"Well, he wasn't exactly singing," said Corporal Sterling. "It was more a chant."

"So," said Doctor Phelps, "what was he chanting?"

"Well," said Corporal Sterling, "it sounded like 'What took you so long?' He kept saying it over and over. 'What took you so long?'"

"That it?"

"Yes."

"Well," said Doctor Phelps, "I got here as soon as I could. I don't know, it could be contagious."

"Exactly *what* could be contagious?" said Ralph Lawton.

By the time Corporal Sterling returned to the Blossom detachment office, Thelma Post was on the phone with Constable Takas. "They got more hard Indians. Sergeant Rogers over at Cardston called, too."

That evening, the channels were filled with reports of petrified Indians turning up all over Canada, the U.S., and parts of South America and Mexico.

"Reports continue to come in," said Knowlton Nash on *The*

National, "of Indians, men, women, and children who have been affected by an unknown form of paralysis. Medical authorities have flown to Arizona to the Navajo reservation where more than six thousand paralyzed Indians have been found."

Doctor Phelps sat in his office and watched the television. He snorted and pushed his lips together. Corporal Sterling sat in a straight-backed chair; a small sack of Bernie's glazed doughnuts sat on the coffee table.

"Paralyzed, my ass," said Doctor Phelps. "Look at this, Corporal. You ever see anything like it?"

Corporal Sterling looked at the Indian lying on the table. The body was glistening.

"What's the matter with him? He looks ... wet."

"Some kind of secretion is my guess. Leaking out all over. Not sticky. All the bodies are getting harder, too. Can't even cut the skin. Look." And Phelps drew his scalpel across the Indian's chest. It made a squeaky sound, but left no mark.

"Whatever it is, it's damn hard." Doctor Phelps went out on his porch and came back with a hammer. "Watch this." He tapped the man's kneecap with the hammer. There was a soft pinging sound.

"You can do it harder, too." And Phelps rapped the man's knee harder. Ping! Ping!

"Paralysis, my ass," said Doctor Phelps, and he hit the Indian's kneecap a savage blow. PING!

For the next month Indians continued to slow down, stiffen up, and turn hard. The six Indians at Doctor Phelps's office had stopped secreting whatever it was they had secreted. The covering over each Indian turned opaque and, later, iridescent.

"Real nice colors," said Corporal Sterling. "What are we going to do with them?"

"Have you heard those damn coyotes?" Doctor Phelps looked out of his office window. The wind was blowing, and the black prairie stubble was beginning to show through the drifts.

"Just the wind," said Corporal Sterling.

"Coyotes," said the Doctor.

"Wind," said the Corporal.

At last count there were one hundred and sixty-four Indians in Blossom, Alberta.

"They look like petrified logs," said Doctor Phelps.

Which gave Corporal Sterling one of the better ideas he had had all year.

"How about we stack them up over at Congistre's warehouse?" he said. "Keep them out of harm's way. If you can't hurt them with that hammer, stacking shouldn't bother them in the least."

"George and Betty Bempo have two standing up in their living room," said Doctor Phelps.

Corporal Sterling frowned. "They do?" he said. "That doesn't seem quite right."

Doctor Phelps shrugged. "Running out of places to put them. They look alright."

Corporal Sterling tried to picture two of the Indians in George and Betty Bempo's living room, and then he called Mike Congistre, who managed Farmer's Wholesale in Blossom.

"It's not contagious, Mike. Only affects Indians. We're running out of space. Maybe we could use part of your warehouse. Got to keep track of them, protect them, you know. Only be for a short time."

Exactly how long, Mike wanted to know.

"Not long," said Corporal Sterling.

By the end of the day, all the stiff Indians in Blossom, Alberta, were stacked ten high in the warehouse.

"Not bad," said Mike. "They stack real good. Now what do we do?"

Which was a very good question.

For the next month, nothing much happened. Corporal Sterling checked on the Indians in the warehouse twice a day.

"You believe those coyotes," said Mike Congistre, as Corporal Sterling played his flashlight over the rigid forms. "What a racket!"

"Thunder," said Corporal Sterling. "Storm must be coming in."

Another month passed.

"Just how long did you say we were going to keep them here?" Mike Congistre wanted to know. "There's no problem during the winter, but we're going to need the space in the spring. How much longer you figure?"

"Soon," said Corporal Sterling. "Soon."

And, as luck would have it, he was right.

On Wednesday of the next week, Corporal Sterling was just finishing his first doughnut when the call came in.

"It's Mike Congistre," said Thelma Post. "He wants to talk with you."

Corporal Sterling leaned forward in his chair and debated whether to have the sugar doughnut or the French cruller next. "Soon," said the Corporal. "Tell him, soon."

Thelma put her hand over the mouthpiece. "He says you better come over to the warehouse. There's a spaceship in the parking lot."

When Corporal Sterling arrived at the warehouse, there was

a large, bright blue spaceship in the parking lot. It looked rather like a doughnut, Corporal Sterling thought, one of the specialty kind that Bernie sometimes made up for a party or an important occasion. Mike Congistre was standing next to the craft.

"What do you think?" said Mike. "It just landed."

"Has anyone come out?"

"No. It's just been sitting there. You figure they're friendly?"

"I'm sure they are," said Corporal Sterling, and he rested his hand on the flap of his shiny dark-brown holster.

Doctor Phelps drove up. "What the hell is it?" he shouted from his car.

"Nothing to worry about," said Corporal Sterling. "Might as well go on home."

"Is it a spaceship?"

"We'll have to wait and see," said Corporal Sterling. "I may have to quarantine this area, too."

"Listen," shouted Doctor Phelps. "I have this theory ..."

But, just then, there was a whirling sound, and part of the ship opened up.

Corporal Sterling turned around. "That's more like it," he said, and he strode over to the entrance and peered into the darkness.

"What do you see?" said Mike Congistre.

"Nothing," said Corporal Sterling, and, as he said it, four medium-sized light-blue things came trotting out of the spaceship. "Stand back," yelled the Corporal. "They could be dangerous."

"They look like coyotes," said Mike Congistre.

"Pets, probably," said Corporal Sterling, and he turned back to the ship. "Good morning," he shouted into the hole. "Welcome to Alberta."

"Hey," said Mike Congistre. "Those coyotes have gone into the warehouse."

"My name is Corporal Colin Sterling of the Royal Canadian Mounted Police. You have landed in Blossom, Alberta, Canada." Corporal Sterling spoke each word slowly and distinctly. "May I be of any assistance?"

Corporal Sterling could not see any movement. The blue was dazzling, and there were little orange lights that spun slowly around the outside of the ship.

"Holy cow!" shouted Mike Congistre.

"Corporal," shouted Doctor Phelps from his car. "Look behind you!"

As Corporal Sterling turned, he saw that each of the four blue coyotes was carrying one of the petrified Indians in its mouth.

"Those blue coyotes have got the Indians," said Mike Congistre.

Corporal Sterling threw his arms out to each side and tried to herd the four coyotes back towards the warehouse. The animals simply trotted past the Corporal and ran onto the ship.

"Did you see that?" said Mike Congistre. "They just took the Indians. You going in after them?"

Corporal Sterling looked at the entrance to the spaceship and rubbed the side of his nose rather violently. "It looks like kidnapping," he said. And he drew his service revolver and walked towards the entrance.

As he got to the entrance, the four animals trotted back out and headed for the warehouse, and Corporal Sterling, as he crept towards the opening with his revolver at the ready, ran into what felt like a sheet of glass.

"Some kind of something ... invisible ... feels like glass," he said. "Stand back, Mr. Congistre." Corporal Sterling took ten paces back, raised his gun, and fired one shot into the barrier. Nothing happened. The bullet just disappeared. He fired a second shot with the same result.

As he fired the second shot, the four blue coyotes came out of the warehouse, each with an Indian in its mouth again.

"Stop!" shouted Corporal Sterling, and he raised a hand. The coyotes trotted around him and into the ship.

"Lock the warehouse," Corporal Sterling shouted. "They are taking our Indians."

Mike Congistre ran to the long galvanized door, dragged it shut, and hooked a massive brass padlock through the hasp. The blue coyotes came out of the ship single file and walked right through the side of the warehouse and reappeared in a few seconds with another four Indians.

"Now what are we going to do?"

"I don't want to shoot them," said Corporal Sterling.

"I don't know if you could," said Mike Congistre.

"If I could just talk to the aliens inside the ship," said Corporal Sterling, "we could probably work this matter out. More than likely, it's not much more than a misunderstanding."

"Maybe they *are* the aliens."

"What? The blue ... dogs?"

"Coyotes."

"Blue alien coyotes?"

Mike Congistre shrugged his shoulders. Doctor Phelps, who had been sitting in his car watching the coyotes carrying the Indians from the warehouse to the ship, came over, all out of breath.

"Did you see those dogs just go through the warehouse wall?"

"They're coyotes," said Corporal Sterling. "Very possibly aliens."

"But did you see that?"

"Of course we saw it," said Corporal Sterling. "The question is, how do we stop them."

"Why?" said Doctor Phelps.

The blue coyotes loped out of the ship and trotted through the warehouse wall again.

"It appears," said Corporal Sterling, "that we are witnessing a rather large kidnapping, and that is against the law."

"But don't you see," said Doctor Phelps. "This must be the reason for the paralysis. The Indians were getting ready for a flight into space."

"Nonsense," said Corporal Sterling. "It's a simple case of kidnapping. What we have here are aliens disguised as blue coyotes who are taking advantage of helpless Indians, who, I might add, are Canadian citizens just like the rest of us here and who are entitled to the same protections as any Canadian gets."

"You don't think they're going to eat them later on or something like that," said Mike Congistre. "I saw a movie once. It was only a movie, of course, but you never know."

The blue coyotes emerged from the building with four more Indians.

"Stop!" said Corporal Sterling, and he grabbed hold of one end of the Indian that the first coyote was carrying. "We'll have none of this." And Corporal Sterling set his feet and began pulling on the Indian.

"It all fits a pattern," said Doctor Phelps. "The paralysis, the airtight and impermeable covering, the spaceship. I'll bet there are ships that have landed all over the place."

"Would you please give me a hand," said Corporal Sterling, who was being dragged towards the ship by the coyote.

"Maybe the Doctor's right," said Mike Congistre. "Maybe we should just let them take the Indians."

The coyote dragged Corporal Sterling headfirst into the invisible barrier.

"You alright?" asked Doctor Phelps.

"I'm fine," said Corporal Sterling, standing up and dusting himself off. "I just need to do some thinking."

"We can go to my office," said Mike Congistre. "It's going to take them a little while to load all the Indians onto the ship."

From the window of the office, Corporal Sterling, Mike Congistre, and Doctor Phelps were able to watch the coyotes go back and forth between the warehouse and the ship.

"I vote we do nothing," said Doctor Phelps.

"This is not an election," said Corporal Sterling. "This is a crime."

"Kinda strange, though," said Mike Congistre. "Like the Doctor says ... more than a coincidence that the Indians would get all hard like that and then these spaceships come along and pick them up. You figure the coyotes are going to eat them?"

"No one is going to eat anyone," said Corporal Sterling. "And no one is going anywhere. Our job is to stop these dogs or coyotes or whatever from taking the Indians."

"That's *your* job," said Doctor Phelps.

"Somebody better do something fast," said Mike Congistre. "They've almost loaded all the Indians."

"There is, of course, a secondary problem which may need to be addressed," said Corporal Sterling. "When they run out of Indians to load on their ship, they could decide to take a few of us, too."

"I doubt there's much danger of that," said Doctor Phelps.

"All of Blossom may be in danger," said Corporal Sterling.

"I think they've loaded the last of the Indians," said Mike Congistre.

Corporal Sterling rose to his feet. "Then," he said, drawing his service revolver again, "I have no alternative."

Corporal Sterling strode out to the parking lot just in time to see the four coyotes running into the ship. "Stop, in the name of the Queen," he shouted, and he aimed his revolver at the ship itself. "Bring back the Indians and surrender yourselves, or I will be forced to fire."

There was a whirling noise, and the entrance to the ship sucked shut.

"I think they're going to leave," yelled Mike Congistre.

Corporal Sterling sighted along the barrel, aiming for one of the flashing orange lights. He fired four times.

The ship rose into the air, hovered for a second over the parking lot, and then disappeared in a flash of blue light.

"Hey," said Mike Congistre, "you scared them away."

"With what?" said Doctor Phelps.

"You may have saved our lives," said Mike Congistre.

"They're probably up there somewhere laughing at us right now," said Doctor Phelps.

"This is not a laughing matter, Doctor Phelps," said Corporal Sterling. "There are kidnapped Canadian citizens on that ship."

"If you ask me," said Doctor Phelps, "they may be better off with the blue coyotes."

"No one asked you," said Corporal Sterling.

That night, on the news, there were reports of spaceships having landed and animals resembling blue dogs loading paralyzed Indians onto the ships.

By the end of the week, all of the petrified Indians in North and South America and Mexico, and other places in the world where you wouldn't expect to find Indians at all, had been loaded onto spaceships.

"They say there were almost fifty Indians that the coyotes picked up over in Germany," said Mike Congistre.

"Probably just there on vacation," said Corporal Sterling.

"I wonder where the spaceships went," said Doctor Phelps.

"Just disappeared, all of them, just like ours did."

"Well, they had to go somewhere," said Doctor Phelps. "What'd that one Indian say again?"

"The one in the motel?"

"Yes."

"The one who sounded like he was singing?"

"Yes."

"He said, 'What took you so long?'"

"See," said Doctor Phelps. "It's just as I thought."

"Anyway," said Mike Congistre, "you stood up to those aliens, Corporal, and for my money, we're probably alive because of your bravery."

"Thank you," said Corporal Colin Sterling, and he broke a cinnamon roll in half and gave Mike the smaller piece. "I just wish I could have saved the Indians, too."

The One
About
Coyote
Going West

This one is about Coyote. She was going west. Visiting her relations. That's what she said. You got to watch that one. Tricky one. Full of bad business. No, no, no, no, that one says. I'm just visiting. Going to see Raven.

Boy, I says. That's another tricky one.

Coyote comes by my place. She wag her tail. Make them happy noises. Sit on my porch. Look around. With them teeth. With that smile. Coyote put her nose in my tea. My good tea.

Get that nose out of my tea, I says.

I'm going to see my friends, she says. Tell those stories. Fix this world. Straighten it up.

Oh boy, pretty scary that, Coyote fix the world, again.

Sit down, I says. Eat some food. Hard work that, fix up the world. Maybe you have a song. Maybe you have a good joke.

Sure, says Coyote. That one wink her ears. Lick her whiskers.

I tuck my feet under that chair. Got to hide my toes. Sometimes that tricky one leave her skin sit in that chair. Coyote skin. No Coyote. Sneak around. Bite them toes. Make you jump.

I been reading those books, she says.

You must be one smart Coyote, I says.

You bet, she says.

Maybe you got a good story for me, I says.

I been reading about that history, says Coyote. She sticks that nose back in my tea. All about who found us Indians.

Ho, I says. I like those old ones. Them ones are the best. You tell me your story, I says. Maybe some biscuits will visit us. Maybe some moose-meat stew come along, listen to your story.

Okay, she says and she sings her story song.

Snow's on the ground the snakes are asleep.
Snow's on the ground my voice is strong.
Snow's on the ground the snakes are asleep.
Snow's on the ground my voice is strong.

She sings like that. With that tail, wagging. With that smile. Sitting there.

Maybe I tell you the one about Eric The Lucky and the Vikings play hockey for the Oldtimers, find us Indians in Newfoundland, she says. Maybe I tell you the one about Christopher Cartier looking for something good to eat. Find us Indians in a restaurant in Montreal. Maybe I tell you the one about Jacques Columbus come along that river. Indians waiting for him. We all wave and say here we are, here we are.

Everyone knows those stories, I says. Whiteman stories. Baby stories you got in your mouth.

No, no, no, no, says that Coyote. I read these ones in that old book.

Ho, I says. You are trying to bite my toes. Everyone knows who found us Indians. Eric The Lucky and that Christopher Cartier and that Jacques Columbus come along later. Those ones get lost. Float about. Walk around. Get mixed up. Ho, ho, ho, ho, those ones cry, we are lost. So we got to find them. Help them out. Feed them. Show them around. Boy, I says. Bad mistake that one.

You are very wise grandmother, says Coyote, bring her eyes down, like she is sleepy. Maybe you know who discovered Indians.

Sure, I says. Everyone knows that. It was Coyote. She was the one.

Oh, grandfather, that Coyote says. Tell me that story. I love those stories about that sneaky one. I don't think I know that story, she says.

Alright, I says. Pay attention.

Coyote was heading west. That's how I always start this story. There was nothing else in this world. Just Coyote. She could see all the way, too. No mountains then. No rivers then. No forests then. Pretty flat then. So she starts to make things. So she starts to fix this world.

This is exciting, says Coyote, and she takes her nose out of my tea.

Yes, I says. Just the beginning, too. Coyote got a lot of things to make.

Tell me, grandmother, says Coyote. What does the clever one make first?

Well, I says. Maybe she makes that tree grows by the river. Maybe she makes that buffalo. Maybe she makes that mountain. Maybe she makes them clouds.

Maybe she makes that beautiful rainbow, says Coyote.

No, I says. She don't make that thing. Mink makes that.

Maybe she makes that beautiful moon, says Coyote.

No, I says. She don't do that either. Otter finds that moon in a pond later on.

Maybe she make the oceans with that blue water, says Coyote.

No, I says. Oceans are already here. She don't do any of that. The first thing Coyote makes, I tell Coyote, is a mistake.

Boy, Coyote sit up straight. Them eyes pop open. That tail stop wagging. That one swallow that smile.

Big one, too, I says. Coyote is going west thinking of things to make. That one is trying to think of everything to make at once. So she don't see that hole. So she falls in that hole. Then those thoughts bump around. They run into each other. Those ones fall out of Coyote's ears. In that hole.

Ho, that Coyote cries. I have fallen into a hole, I must have made a mistake. And she did.

So there is that hole. And there is that Coyote in that hole. And there is that big mistake in that hole with Coyote. Ho, says that mistake. You must be Coyote.

That mistake is real big and that hole is small. Not much room. I don't want to tell you what that mistake looks like. First mistake in the world. Pretty scary. Boy, I can't look, I got to close my eyes. You better close your eyes, too, I tell Coyote.

Okay, I'll do that, she says, and she puts her hands over her eyes. But she don't fool me. I can see she's peeking.

Don't peek, I says.

Okay, she says. I won't do that.

Well you know, that Coyote thinks about the hole. And she thinks about how she's going to get out of that hole. She thinks how she's going to get that big mistake back in her head.

Say, says that mistake. What is that you're thinking about?

I'm thinking of a song, says Coyote. I'm thinking of a song to make this hole bigger.

That's a good idea, says that mistake. Let me hear your hole song.

But that's not what Coyote sings. She sings a song to make the mistake smaller. But that mistake hears her. And that mistake grabs Coyote's nose. And that one pulls off her mouth so she can't sing. And that one jumps up and down on Coyote until she is flat. Then that one leaps out of that hole, wanders around looking for things to do.

Well, Coyote is feeling pretty bad all flat her nice fur coat full of stomp holes. So she thinks hard, and she thinks about a healing song. And she tries to sing a healing song, but her mouth is in other places. So she thinks harder and tries to sing that song through her nose. But that nose don't make any sound, just drip a lot. She tries to sing that song out her ears, but those ears don't hear anything.

So, that silly one thinks real hard and tries to sing out her butt hole. Pssst! Pssst! That is what that butt hole says, and right away things don't smell so good in that hole. Pssst.

Boy, Coyote thinks. Something smells.

That Coyote lies there flat and practice and practice. Pretty soon, maybe two days, maybe one year, she teach that butt hole to sing. That song. That healing song. So that butt hole sings that song. And Coyote begins to feel better. And Coyote don't feel so flat anymore. Pssst! Pssst! Things smell pretty bad, but Coyote is okay.

That one look around in that hole. Find her mouth. Put that

mouth back. So, she says to that butt hole. Okay, you can stop singing now. You can stop making them smells now. But, you know, that butt hole is liking all that singing, and so that butt hole keeps on singing.

Stop, says Coyote. You are going to stink up the whole world. But it don't. So Coyote jumps out of that hole and runs across the prairies real fast. But that butt hole follows her. Pssst. Pssst. Coyote jumps into a lake, but that butt hole don't drown. It just keeps on singing.

Hey, who is doing all that singing, someone says.

Yes, and who is making that bad smell, says another voice.

It must be Coyote, says a third voice.

Yes, says a fourth voice. I believe it is Coyote.

That Coyote sit in my chair, put her nose in my tea, say, I know who that voice is. It is that big mistake playing a trick. Nothing else is made yet.

No, I says. That mistake is doing other things.

Then those voices are spirits, says Coyote.

No, I says. Them voices belong to them ducks.

Coyote stand up on my chair. Hey, she says, where did them ducks come from?

Calm down, I says. This story is going to be okay. This story is doing just fine. This story knows where it is going. Sit down. Keep your skin on.

So.

Coyote look around, and she see them four ducks. In that lake. Ho, she says. Where did you ducks come from? I didn't make you yet.

Yes, says them ducks. We were waiting around, but you didn't come. So we got tired of waiting. So we did it ourselves.

I was in a hole, says Coyote.

Pssst. Pssst.

What's that noise, says them ducks. What's that bad smell?

Never mind, says Coyote. Maybe you've seen something go by. Maybe you can help me find something I lost. Maybe you can help me get it back.

Those ducks swim around and talk to themselves. Was it something awful to look at?

Yes, says Coyote, it certainly was.

Was it something with ugly fur?

Yes, says Coyote. I think it had that, too.

Was it something that made a lot of noise, ask them ducks.

Yes, it was pretty noisy, says Coyote.

Did it smell bad, them ducks want to know.

Yes, says Coyote. I guess you ducks have seen my something.

Yes, says them ducks. It is right there behind you.

So that Coyote turn around, and there is nothing there.

It's still behind you, says those ducks.

So Coyote turn around again but she don't see anything.

Pssst! Pssst!

Boy, says those ducks. What a noise! What a smell! They say that, too. What an ugly thing with all that fur!

Never mind, says that Coyote again. That is not what I'm looking for. I'm looking for something else.

Maybe you're looking for Indians, says those ducks.

Well, that Coyote is real surprised because she hasn't created Indians, either. Boy, says that one, mischief is everywhere. This world is getting bent.

Alright.

So Coyote and those ducks are talking, and pretty soon they hear a noise. And pretty soon there is something coming. And those ducks says, oh, oh, oh, oh. They say that like they see trouble, but it is not trouble. What comes along is a river.

Hello, says that river. Nice day. Maybe you want to take a swim. But Coyote don't want to swim, and she looks at that river and she looks at that river again. Something's not right here, she says. Where are those rocks? Where are those rapids? What did you do with them waterfalls? How come you're so straight?

And Coyote is right. That river is nice and straight and smooth without any bumps or twists. It runs both ways, too, not like a modern river.

We got to fix this, says Coyote, and she does. She puts some rocks in that river, and she fixes it so it only runs one way. She puts a couple of waterfalls in and makes a bunch of rapids where things get shallow fast.

Coyote is tired with all this work, and those ducks are tired just watching. So that Coyote sits down. So she closes her eyes. So she puts her nose in her tail. So those ducks shout, wake up, wake up! Something big is heading this way! And they are right.

Mountain come sliding along, whistling. Real happy mountain. Nice and round. This mountain is full of grapes and other good things to eat. Apples, peaches, cherries. Howdy-do, says that polite mountain, nice day for whistling.

Coyote looks at that mountain, and that one shakes her head. Oh no, she says, this mountain is all wrong. How come you're so nice and round. Where are those craggy peaks? Where are all them cliffs? What happened to all that snow? Boy, we got to fix this thing, too. So she does.

Grandfather, grandfather, says that Coyote, sit in my chair put her nose in my tea. Why is that Coyote changing all those good things?

That is a real sly one, ask me that question. I look at those eyes. Grab them ears. Squeeze that nose. Hey, let go my nose, that Coyote says.

Okay, I says. Coyote still in Coyote skin. I bet you know why Coyote change that happy river. Why she change that mountain sliding along whistling.

No, says that Coyote, look around my house, lick her lips, make them baby noises.

Maybe it's because she is mean, I says.

Oh no, says Coyote. That one is sweet and kind.

Maybe it's because that one is not too smart.

Oh no, says Coyote. That Coyote is very wise.

Maybe it's because she made a mistake.

Oh no, says Coyote. She made one of those already.

Alright, I says. Then Coyote must be doing the right thing. She must be fixing up the world so it is perfect.

Yes, says Coyote. That must be it. What does that brilliant one do next?

Everyone knows what Coyote does next, I says. Little babies know what Coyote does next.

Oh no, says Coyote. I have never heard this story. You are a wonderful storyteller. You tell me your good Coyote story.

Boy, you got to watch that one all the time. Hide them toes.

Well, I says. Coyote thinks about that river. And she thinks about that mountain. And she thinks somebody is fooling around. So she goes looking around. She goes looking for that one who is messing up the world.

She goes to the north, and there is nothing. She goes to the south, and there is nothing there either. She goes to the east, and there is still nothing there. She goes to the west, and there is a pile of snow tires.

And there is some televisions. And there is some vacuum cleaners. And there is a bunch of pastel sheets. And there is an air humidifier. And there is a big mistake sitting on a portable gas barbecue reading a book. Big book. Department store catalog.

Hello, says that mistake. Maybe you want a hydraulic jack.

No, says that Coyote. I don't want one of them. But she don't tell that mistake what she wants because she don't want to miss her mouth again. But when she thinks about being flat and full of stomp holes, that butt hole wakes up and begins to sing. Pssst. Pssst.

What's that noise, says that big mistake.

I'm looking for Indians, says that Coyote real quick. Have you seen any?

What's that bad smell?

Never mind, says Coyote. Maybe you have some Indians around here.

I got some toaster ovens, says that mistake.

We don't need that stuff, says Coyote. You got to stop making all those things. You're going to fill up this world.

Maybe you want a computer with a color monitor. That mistake keeps looking through that book and those things keep landing in piles all around Coyote.

Stop, stop, cries Coyote. Golf cart lands on her foot. Golf balls bounce off her head. You got to give me that book before the world gets lopsided.

These are good things, says that mistake. We need these things to make up the world. Indians are going to need this stuff.

We don't have any Indians, says that Coyote.

And that mistake can see that that's right. Maybe we better

make some Indians, says that mistake. So that one looks in that catalog, but it don't have any Indians. And Coyote don't know how to do that either. She has already made four things.

I've made four things already, she says. I got to have help.

We can help, says some voices and it is those ducks come swimming along. We can help you make Indians, says that white duck. Yes, we can do that, says that green duck. We have been thinking about this, says that blue duck. We have a plan, says that red duck.

Well, that Coyote don't know what to do. So she tells the ducks to go ahead because this story is pretty long and it's getting late and everyone wants to go home.

You still awake, I says to Coyote. You still here?

Oh yes, grandmother, says Coyote. What do those clever ducks do?

So I tell Coyote that those ducks lay some eggs. Ducks do that you know. That white duck lay an egg, and it is blue. That red duck lay an egg, and it is green. That blue duck lay an egg, and it is red. That green duck lay an egg, and it is white.

Come on, says those ducks. We got to sing a song. We got to do a dance. So they do. Coyote and that big mistake and those four ducks dance around the eggs. So they dance and sing for a long time, and pretty soon Coyote gets hungry.

I know this dance, she says, but you got to close your eyes when you do it or nothing will happen. You got to close your eyes tight. Okay, says those ducks. We can do that. And they do. And that big mistake closes its eyes, too.

But Coyote, she don't close her eyes, and all of them start dancing again, and Coyote dances up close to that white duck, and she grabs that white duck by her neck.

When Coyote grabs that duck, that duck flaps her wings, and that big mistake hears the noise and opens them eyes. Say, says that big mistake, that's not the way the dance goes.

By golly, you're right, says Coyote, and she lets that duck go. I am getting it mixed up with another dance.

So they start to dance again. And Coyote is very hungry, and she grabs that blue duck, and she grabs his wings, too. But Coyote's stomach starts to make hungry noises, and that mistake opens them eyes and sees Coyote with the blue duck. Hey, says that mistake, you got yourself mixed up again.

That's right, says Coyote, and she drops that duck and straightens out that neck. It sure is good you're around to help me with this dance.

They all start that dance again, and, this time, Coyote grabs the green duck real quick and tries to stuff it down that greedy throat, and there is nothing hanging out but them yellow duck feet. But those feet are flapping in Coyote's eyes, and she can't see where she is going, and she bumps into the big mistake and the big mistake turns around to see what has happened.

Ho, says that big mistake, you can't see where you're going with them yellow duck feet flapping in your eyes, and that mistake pulls that green duck out of Coyote's throat. You could hurt yourself dancing like that.

You are one good friend, look after me like that, says Coyote.

Those ducks start to dance again, and Coyote dances with them, but that red duck says, we better dance with one eye open, so we can help Coyote with this dance. So they dance some more, and then, those eggs begin to move around, and those eggs crack open. And if you look hard, you can see something inside those eggs.

I know, I know, says that Coyote jump up and down on my chair, shake up my good tea. Indians come out of those eggs. I remember this story, now. Inside those eggs are the Indians Coyote's been looking for.

No, I says. You are one crazy Coyote. What comes out of those duck eggs are baby ducks. You better sit down, I says. You may fall and hurt yourself. You may spill my tea. You may fall on top of this story and make it flat.

Where are the Indians, says that Coyote. This story was about how Coyote found the Indians. Maybe the Indians are in the eggs with the baby ducks.

No, I says, nothing in those eggs but little baby ducks. Indians will be along in a while. Don't lose your skin.

So.

When those ducks see what has come out of the eggs, they says, boy, we didn't get that quite right. We better try that again. So they do. They lay them eggs. They dance that dance. They sing that song. Those eggs crack open and out comes some more baby ducks. They do this seven times and each time, they get more ducks.

By golly, says those four ducks. We got more ducks than we need. I guess we got to be the Indians. And so they do that. Before Coyote or that big mistake can mess things up, those four ducks turn into Indians, two women and two men. Good-looking Indians, too. They don't look at all like ducks anymore.

But those duck-Indians aren't too happy. They look at each other and they begin to cry. This is pretty disgusting, they says. All this ugly skin. All these bumpy bones. All this awful black hair. Where are our nice soft feathers? Where are our beautiful feet? What happened to our wonderful wings? It's probably all that Coyote's fault because she didn't do the dance right, and those four duck-Indians come over and stomp all over Coyote until she is flat like before. Then they leave. That big mistake leave, too. And that Coyote, she starts to think about a healing song.

Pssst. Pssst.

That's it, I says. It is done.

But what happens to Coyote, says Coyote. That wonderful one is still flat.

Some of these stories are flat, I says. That's what happens when you try to fix this world. This world is pretty good all by itself. Best to leave it alone. Stop messing around with it.

I better get going, says Coyote. I will tell Raven your good story. We going to fix this world for sure. We know how to do it, now. We know how to do it right.

So, Coyote drinks my tea and that one leave. And I can't talk anymore because I got to watch the sky. Got to watch out for falling things that land in piles. When that Coyote's wandering around looking to fix things, nobody in this world is safe.

A Seat
in the
Garden

Joe Hovaugh settled into the garden on his knees and began pulling at the wet, slippery weeds that had sprung up between the neat rows of beets. He trowelled his way around the zucchini and up and down the lines of carrots, and he did not notice the big Indian at all until he stopped at the tomatoes, sat back, and tried to remember where he had set the ball of twine and the wooden stakes.

The big Indian was naked to the waist. His hair was braided and wrapped with white ermine and strips of red cloth. He wore a single feather held in place by a leather band stretched around his head, and, even though his arms were folded tightly across his chest, Joe could see the glitter and flash of silver and turquoise on each finger.

"If you build it, they will come," said the big Indian.

Joe rolled forward and shielded his eyes from the morning sun.

"If you build it, they will come," said the big Indian again.

"Christ sakes," Joe shouted. "Get the hell out of the corn, will ya!"

"If you build it ..."

"Yeah, yeah. Hey! This is private property. You people ever hear of private property?"

" ... they will come."

Joe struggled to his feet and got his shovel from the shed. But when he got back to the garden, the big Indian was gone.

"Alright!" Joe shouted and drove the nose of the shovel into the ground. "Come out of that corn!"

The corn stalks were only about a foot tall. Nevertheless, Joe walked each row, the shovel held at the ready just in case the big Indian tried to take him by surprise.

When Red Mathews came by in the afternoon, Joe poured him a cup of coffee and told him about the big Indian and what he had said, and Red told Joe that he had seen the movie.

"Wasn't a movie, Red, damn it. It was a real Indian. He was just standing there in the corn."

"You probably scared him away."

"You can't let them go standing in your garden whenever they feel like it."

"That's the truth."

The next day, when Joe came out to the garden to finish staking the tomatoes, the big Indian was waiting for him. The man looked as though he was asleep, but, as soon as he saw Joe, he straightened up and crossed his arms on his chest.

"You again!"

"If you build it ..."

"I'm going to call the police. You hear me. The police are going to come and haul you away."

" ... they will come."

Joe turned around and marched back into the house and phoned the RCMP, who said they would send someone over that very afternoon.

"Afternoon? What am I supposed to do with him until then. Feed him lunch?"

The RCMP officer told Joe that it might be best if he stayed in his house. There was the chance, the officer said, that the big Indian might be drunk or on drugs and, if that were the case, it was better if Joe didn't antagonize him.

"He's walking on my corn. Does that mean anything to you?"

The RCMP officer assured Joe that it meant a great deal to him, that his wife was a gardener, and he knew how she would feel if someone walked on her corn.

"Still," said the officer, "it's best if you don't do anything."

What Joe did do was to call Red, and, when Red arrived, the big Indian was still in the garden waiting.

"Wow, he's a big sucker, alright," said Red. "You know, he looks a little like Jeff Chandler."

"I called the police, and they said not to antagonize him."

"Hey, there are two of us, right?"

"That's right," said Joe.

"You bet it's right."

Joe got the shovel and a hoe from the shed, and he and Red wandered out into the garden as if nothing was wrong.

"He's watching us," said Red.

"Don't step on the tomatoes," said Joe.

Joe walked around the zucchini, casually dragging the shovel behind him. Red ambled through the beets, the hoe slung over his shoulder.

"If you build it, they will come."

"Get him!" shouted Joe. And before Red could do anything, Joe was charging through the carrots, the shovel held out in front like a lance.

"Wait a minute, Joe," yelled Red, the hoe still on his shoulder. But Joe was already into the tomatoes. He was closing on the big Indian, who hadn't moved, when he stepped on the bundle of wooden stakes and went down in a heap.

"Hey," said Red. "You okay?"

Red helped Joe to his feet, and, when the two men looked around, the big Indian was gone.

"Where'd he go?" said Joe.

"Beats me," said Red. "What'd you do to get him so angry?"

Red helped Joe to the house, wrapped an ice pack on his ankle, and told him to put his leg on the chair.

"I saw a movie a couple of years back about a housing development that was built on top of an ancient Indian burial mound."

"I would have got him, if I hadn't tripped."

"They finally had to get an authentic medicine man to come in and appease the spirits."

"Did you see the look on his face when he saw me coming?"

"And you should have seen some of those spirits."

When the RCMP arrived, Joe showed the officer where the Indian had stood, how he had run at him with the shovel, and how he had stumbled over the bundle of stakes.

After Joe got up and brushed himself off, the RCMP officer asked him if he recognized the big Indian.

"Not likely," said Joe. "There aren't any Indians around here."

"Yes, there are," said Red. "Remember those three guys who come around on weekends every so often."

"The old winos?" said Joe.

"They have that grocery cart, and they pick up cans."

"They don't count."

"They sit down there by the hydrangea and crush the cans and eat their lunch. Sometimes they get to singing."

"You mean drink their lunch."

"Well, they could have anything in that bottle."

"Most likely Lysol."

The RCMP officer walked through the garden with Joe and Red and made a great many notes. He shook hands with both men and told Joe to call him if there was any more trouble.

"Did you ever wonder," said Red, after the officer left, "just what he wants you to build or who 'they' are?"

"I suppose you saw a movie."

"Maybe we should ask the Indians."

"The drunks?"

"Maybe they could translate for us."

"The guy speaks English."

"That's right, Joe. God, this gets stranger all the time. Ed Ames, that's who he reminds me of."

On Saturday morning, when Joe and Red walked out on the porch, the big Indian was waiting patiently for them in the corn. They were too far away to hear him, but they could see his mouth moving.

"Okay," said Red. "All we got to do is wait for the Indians to show up."

The Indians showed up around noon. One man had a green knapsack. The other two pushed a grocery cart in front of them. It was full of cans and bottles. They were old, Joe noticed, and even from the porch, he imagined he could smell them. They walked to a corner of the garden behind the hydrangea where the sprinklers didn't reach. It was a dry, scraggly wedge that Joe had never bothered to cultivate. As soon as the men stopped the cart and sat down on the ground, Red got to his feet and stretched.

"Come on. Can't hurt to talk with them. Grab a couple of beers, so they know we're friendly."

"A good whack with the shovel would be easier."

"Hey, this is kind of exciting. Don't you think this is kind of exciting?"

"I wouldn't trip this time."

When Joe and Red got to the corner, the three men were busy crushing the cans. One man would put a can on a flat stone and the second man would step on it. The third man picked up the crushed can and put it in a brown grocery bag. They were older than Joe had thought, and they didn't smell as bad as he had expected.

"Hi," said Red. "That's a nice collection of cans."

"Good morning," said the first Indian.

"Getting pretty hot," said the second Indian.

"You fellows like a drink?" said the third Indian, and he took a large glass bottle out of the knapsack.

"No thanks," said Red. "You fellows like a beer?"

"Lemon water," said the third Indian. "My wife makes it without any sugar so it's not as sweet as most people like."

"How can you guys drink that stuff?" said Joe.

"You get used to it," said the second Indian. "And it's better for you than pop."

As the first Indian twisted the lid off the bottle and took a long drink, Joe looked around to make sure none of his neighbors were watching him.

"I'll bet you guys know just about everything there is to know about Indians," said Red.

"Well," said the first Indian, "Jimmy and Frank are Nootka and I'm Cree. You guys reporters or something?"

"Reporters? No."

"You never know," said the second Indian. "Last month, a couple of reporters did a story on us. Took pictures and everything."

"It's good that these kinds of problems are brought to the public's attention," said Red.

"You bet," said the third Indian. "Everyone's got to help. Otherwise there's going to be more garbage than people."

Joe was already bored with the conversation. He looked back to see if the big Indian was still there.

"This is all nice and friendly," said Joe. "But we've got a problem that we were hoping you might be able to help us with."

"Sure," said the first Indian. "What's the problem?"

Joe snapped the tab on one of the beers, took a long swig, and jerked his thumb in the direction of the garden. "I've got this big Indian who likes to stand in my garden."

"Where?" asked the second Indian.

"Right there," said Joe.

"Right where?" asked the third Indian.

"If you build it, they will come," shouted the big Indian.

"There, there," said Joe. "Did you hear that?"

"Hear what?" said the first Indian.

"They're embarrassed," said Red under his breath. "Let me handle this."

"This is beginning to piss me off," said Joe, and he took another pull on the beer.

"We were just wondering," Red began. "If you woke up one day and found a big Indian standing in your cornfield and all he would say was, 'If you build it, they will come,' what would you do?"

"I'd stop drinking," said the second Indian, and the other two Indians covered their faces with their hands.

"No, no," said Red. "That's not what I mean. Well ... you see that big Indian over there in the cornfield, don't you?"

The Indians looked at each other, and then they looked at Joe and Red.

"Okay," said the first Indian. "Sure, I see him."

"Oh, yeah," said the second Indian. "He's right there, all right. In the ... beets?"

"Corn," said Joe.

"Right," said the third Indian. "In the corn. I can see him, too. Clear as day."

"That's our problem," said Red. "We think maybe he's a spirit or something."

"No, we don't," said Joe.

"Yes, we do," said Red, who was just getting going. "We figure he wants us to build something to appease him so he'll go away."

"Sort of like ... a spirit?" said the first Indian.

"Hey," said the second Indian, "remember that movie we saw about that community that was built ..."

"That's the one," said Red. "What we have to figure out is what he wants us to build. You guys got any ideas?"

The three Indians looked at each other. The first Indian looked at the cornfield. Then he looked at Joe and Red.

"Tell you what," he said. "We'll go over there and talk to him and see what he wants. He looks ... Cree. You guys stay here, okay."

Joe and Red watched as the three Indians walked into the garden. They stood together facing the beets.

"Hey," shouted Joe. "You guys blind? He's behind you."

The first Indian waved his hand and smiled, and the three men turned around. Red could see them talking, and he tried to watch their lips, but he couldn't figure out what they were saying. After a while, the Indians waved at the rows of carrots and came back over to where Joe and Red were waiting.

"Well," said Red. "Did you talk to him?"

"Yes," said the first Indian. "You were right. He is a spirit."

"I knew it!" shouted Red. "What does he want?"

The first Indian looked back to the cornfield. "He's tired of standing, he says. He wants a place to sit down. But he doesn't want to mess up the garden. He says he would like it if you would build him a ... a ... bench right about ... here."

"A bench?" said Joe.

"That's what he said."

"So he can sit down?"

"He gets tired standing."

"The hell you say."

"Do you still see him?" asked the second Indian.

"You blind? Of course I still see him."

"Then I'd get started on the bench right away," said the third Indian.

"Come on, Red," said Joe, and he threw the empty beer can into the hydrangea and opened the other one. "We got to talk."

Joe put the pad of paper on the kitchen table and drew a square. "This is the garden," he said. "These are the carrots. These are the beets. These are the beans. And this is the corn. The big Indian is right about here."

"That's right," said Red. "But what does it mean?"

"Here's where those winos crush their cans and drink their Lysol," Joe continued, marking a spot on the pad and drawing a line to it.

"Lemon water."

"You listening?"

"Sure."

"If you draw lines from the house to where the big Indian stands and from there to where the winos crush their cans and back to the house ... Now do you see it?"

"Hey, that's pretty good, Joe."

"What does it remind you of?"

"A bench?"

"No," said Joe. "A triangle."

"Okay, I can see that."

"And if you look at it like this, you can see clearly that the winos and the big Indian are there, and the house where you and I are is here."

"What if you looked at it this way, Joe," said Red and he turned the paper a half turn to the right. "Now the house is there and the old guys and the big Indian are here."

"That's not the way you look at it. That's not the way it works."

"Does that mean we're not going to build the bench?"

"It's our battle plan."

"A bench might be simpler," said Red.

"I'll attack him from the house along this line. You take

him from the street along that line. We'll catch him between
us."

"I don't know that this is going to work."

"Just don't step on the tomatoes."

The next morning, Red waited behind the hydrangea. He
was carrying the hoe and a camera. Joe crouched by the corner
of the house with the shovel.

"Charge!" yelled Joe, and he broke from his hiding place
and lumbered across the yard and into the garden. Red leaped
through the hydrangea and struggled up the slight incline to
the cornfield.

"If you build it, they will come," shouted the Indian.

"Build it yourself," shouted Joe, and he swung the shovel
at the big Indian's legs. Red, who was slower, stopped at the
edge of the cornfield to watch Joe whack the Indian with his
shovel and to take a picture, so he saw Joe and his shovel run
right through the Indian and crash into the compost
mound.

"Joe, Joe ... you alright? God, you should have seen it. You
ran right through that guy. Just like he wasn't there. I got a
great picture. Wait till you see the picture. Just around the
eyes, he looks a little like Sal Mineo."

Red helped Joe back to the house and cleaned the cuts on
Joe's face. He wrapped another ice pack on Joe's ankle and
then drove down to the one-hour photo store and turned the
film in. By the time he got back to the house, Joe was standing on the porch, leaning on the railing.

"You won't believe it, Joe," said Red. "Look at this."

Red fished a photograph out of the pack. It showed Joe and
the shovel in mid-swing, plunging through the corn. The
colors were brilliant.

Joe looked at the photograph for a minute and then he looked at the cornfield. "Where's the big Indian?"

"That's just it. He's not there."

"Christ!"

"Does that mean we're going to build the bench?"

The bench was a handsome affair with a concrete base and a wooden seat. The Indians came by the very next Saturday with their knapsack and grocery cart, and Red could tell that they were impressed.

"Boy," said the first Indian, "that's a good-looking bench."

"You think this will take care of the problem?" asked Red.

"That Indian still in the cornfield?" said the second Indian.

"Of course he's still there," said Joe. "Can't you hear him?"

"I don't know," said the third Indian, and he twisted the lid off the bottle and took a drink. "I don't think he's one of ours."

"What should we do?"

"Don't throw your cans in the hydrangea," said the first Indian. "It's hard to get them out. We're not as young as we used to be."

Joe and Red spent the rest of the day sitting on the porch, drinking beer, and watching the big Indian in the garden. He looked a little like Victor Mature, Red thought, now that he had time to think about it, or maybe Anthony Quinn, only he was taller. And there was an air about the man that made Red believe—believe with all his heart—that he had met this Indian before.

Joe
the Painter
and the
Deer Island
Massacre

Joe the Painter knew almost everyone in town and everyone knew Joe and all of the people who knew Joe as well as I knew Joe didn't like him. Except me. I liked Joe. I was probably the only person who was willing to be seen with Joe regular like. A lot of folk would say hi to Joe if they ran into him and couldn't get across the street in time and some would even sit down to coffee with him while the sun was out. One or two of the married fellows had invited Joe to dinner at their houses but they only did it once.

Joe was friendly enough. Whenever he'd see someone he knew, he'd boom out a "Howdy."

"Howdy Ed," he shouted at Ed Petersen as Ed slipped out of the old Vance hotel at three in the afternoon. Joe was friendly like that. "What the hell you doing in the Vance at this time of the day?"

But he wasn't one to chew his words.

"Dingdang! George, don't tell me you actually paid $5,000 for that piece of junk?"

He was polite. He just wasn't judicious.

"Howdy Mrs. Secord, how's the girls? Looks like you been living off pudding. Say, you pregnant again? Damn fine weather ain't it."

"Joe's just an honest man," Marvin Booster, the bartender at the Ritz, would tell his customers after Joe left. "Most people can't manage honesty. Honesty makes most people nervous."

"Howdy Marvin, you settle up with the tax boys yet?"

Joe just had a habit of making people uncomfortable. Most times they would try and drift away before Joe stuck them with one of his "howdies."

"Howdy Bill, did you beat the drunk driving ticket?"

"Howdy Pete, you and the Mrs. back together yet?"

"Howdy Betty, god you look like hell. You had a relapse?"

But that wasn't exactly why people avoided Joe though it was a pretty good reason all by itself. And it wasn't that he was dirty or smelled bad. He took a shower every morning and his clothes were always clean. He didn't drink. And he didn't smoke.

"Howdy Bob, you know a bullet would be a heck of a lot faster and not near the expense."

Joe didn't like smoking at all.

"Smoking just touches me wrong though I suppose I got a few bad habits, too."

Joe liked to blow his nose in the gutter. Whenever he felt a clog in his "breathing trap" as he called it, he'd step to the curb, lean over so as not to get his shoes dirty, hold one nostril shut with his thumb, snort, and blow out the other one. Then he'd change hands. Like shooting beans through a straw. He always did it first thing in the morning and then, after that, whenever the occasion demanded it.

On weekends, sometimes, a few of the kids on their way to

the docks to fish would hang around in front of the Ritz bar and wait for Joe to come down from his bachelor apartment. He'd blow a little louder for the kids.

I think that Joe's main problem was that he was loud. He wasn't boisterous, he just talked loud all the time. Maybe he was a bit deaf and didn't want to admit it or just didn't know it. Before he came out to the coast, he had worked in a foundry back east.

"It was real noisy," Joe shouted. And he liked to stand close to you when he talked. It was no good backing up because he'd just follow you around until he got you in a corner.

People who disliked Joe didn't dislike him because he was a criminal or snobbish or weird or perverted or mean, it was a whole bunch of things that altogether tended to overwhelm folk.

"You're probably the only friend, only real friend that Joe the Painter has," Howard Souto told me once and I suppose he was right.

I liked Joe. He was a friend to me and a good one.

Joe's real name was Joseph Ghoti. Everyone just called him Joe or Joe the Painter because he had painted houses for a living before he retired and moved into the small apartment above the Ritz.

The one thing that no one could fault Joe for was his civic spirit. He went to all the political rallies ... for both parties. He voted in all the elections and if he felt particularly strong about some issue, he'd paint a paper placard and hang it out of his apartment window. He bought poppies on Veterans Day, kept his old papers and pop bottles for the Boy Scouts and bought dozens of boxes of Girl Scout cookies and gave them away as presents to the kids who stopped by on their way to the wharf. He went to the county fair every year and stood when they played the National Anthem. He'd even stand when they played it on television. I watched a baseball game with him once that was played in Montreal and he stood when they played the Canadian National Anthem.

"That's the Canadian National Anthem," shouted Joe as he jumped out of his chair. "Come on, stand up and get your hat off, those folks got feelings too you know."

It was his civic spirit that seemed to get him into most of his trouble.

About three years ago Joe caught me on the street just outside Lazio's Marine Supply store.

"Howdy Chief," shouted Joe. "You got time for coffee? Something in the paper you ought to see."

Joe was the only one in town called me Chief. My family was from Horseshoe Bar, a mountain community about seventy miles out of town. My father was Cherokee, out of Oklahoma during the dust bowl years. He had settled in at Horseshoe Bar and married a Pomo woman up from Round Valley. I wasn't a chief and Joe knew it but he didn't smile when he said it.

"Look at this ... right there ... what do you think?"

"Where?"

"There, there ... right there," Joe shouted and stabbed his finger into the paper.

"The centennial celebration?"

"That's it. How about that! The town's one hundred years old."

"That's great, Joe." I said it without much inflection.

"Great? Can't you read? Look here. There's going to be a competition for the best pageant."

"That's great, Joe."

"What's the matter? Hey, maybe you don't know what a pageant is, huh? Is that it? Maybe you can't read." And he stabbed the paper again.

"So ... there's going to be a pageant. That's great."

"Damn, I guess I'm going to have to read it to you."

There was no stopping Joe once he got started.

"'The city council announced last night,'" Joe began loud enough to be heard down the street in the Ritz, "'that the California State Endowment for the Arts has approved the city's application for $56,000. The money will be used to stage a pageant competition. The successful pageant will be performed as part of the centennial celebration. Applications for the pageant competition should be ready at City Hall by the end of the week.' Maybe now you're more excited."

"What's to get excited about. Hell, Joe, what are we going to do, enter the pageant competition?"

"Now you're talking!"

"A pageant?"

"Sure, be a great thing to do for the town. Give the town a pageant that would do it proud. And you get paid. See ... right here ... 'participants in the successful pageant will be paid for their performances during the month of April.' You got performances four nights with two performances on Friday and Saturday ... for a whole month."

"Where are we going to get a pageant?"

"Well, you just don't go out to your local market and buy one. Damn, you don't just walk up to Howard Souto at the Green Front and say, "Howdy, Howard, got any ripe pageants in today?"

"Joe ..."

"You got to write one!"

"Joe ..."

"A pageant about the way this town was founded. That would win the competition. I could write it, you know. What do you think?"

My coffee was getting cold.

"Why would you want to write a pageant?"

"Why? Chief, I live here. This is a good town. Damn fine town. And it's going to have a birthday, you know. And I can write a real good pageant and do it up right. This is my town. Who else should write a pageant?"

"Well, sure as hell not me," I said, trying to get a taste of my coffee.

"Dingdang, of course not you. You can't write. You can hardly read and I suspect that you don't even know exactly what a pageant is. Besides, you're going to be one of the stars."

"One of the stars?"

"That's right ... Ah-ha, now you're interested."

"You're nuts, Joe ... I'm no pageant-er or whatever I'd be."

"An actor ... a star!"

"Forget it. You can write your pageant and I'll watch it and I'll bring my family, bring everyone up at the Bar and we'll all cheer when it's over but I won't be in it."

"Look Chief," said Joe seriously, bringing his voice down to a normal volume which meant he was going to tell me a secret. "My pageant is going to have Indians in it. You're the only Indian I know."

"I can get you lots of Indians."

"And," said Joe, reaching across and patting my hand, "you're my best friend."

Well, hell, what was I supposed to say?

I didn't see Joe after that for near a week. He caught up with me over a cup of coffee and pie at Connie's.

"Howdy Chief," Joe sang out, waving a piece of paper around in a circle.

Ed Petersen, who was sitting at the counter, slid off the stool and headed for the rest room. Bill Johnson left half a cup of good hot coffee, dropped a dollar at the register, and left before Connie could give him his change. Mrs. Bertrand, sitting at the front booth, disappeared behind a copy of the *Herald*.

"Howdy, Connie, how's the boil doing?"

Joe slid in across from me and slapped the paper down on the table.

"There's this screening," he shouted. "You have to submit an idea for the pageant. Council's got this jury that is going to look at all the ideas and select the best three."

"They going to do all three pageants?"

"Chief, you're not listening again. The jury is going to choose three. Whoever gets chosen will get a small grant. You take the grant, work up the pageant, and about a month before the centennial celebration, the city council will preview each pageant and choose the best one. That pageant will be the one that is shown during the centennial."

"Oh." I could see that I was going to need more coffee.

"You awake? You got all that?"

"Sure, but what do I have to do?"

"I'll be the author ... been doing some research and I've got the idea right here," and he tapped his head to indicate the general location. "I need you to get me thirty or forty Indians. All kinds ... you know, men, women, and kids ... could use lots of kids."

"Thirty or forty?"

"How many in your family?"

"Two brothers and three sisters."

"That won't be enough. You got any friends besides me?"

"Indians?"

"Chief, you hard of hearing ... we been talking about Portuguese fishermen? Course I mean Indians. I need thirty or forty Indians."

There was my father and his two brothers and their families at the Bar and Bernie and James and their cousins over at Hupa Valley. Mom had a couple of sisters down south who might come up.

"I suppose."

"Don't be supposing, supposing killed the cat."

"What's the pageant going to be about?"

"Can't tell, it's a secret."

"Suppose you tell me."

"There you go supposing again."

"You don't know yet, huh?"

"Dingdang, course I know. Say, are you trying to wring my leg out? Damned if I don't think sometimes you're dumber than you look."

"How about a hint? Got to tell the folks something."

"Stay right there," Joe shouted, sliding out of the booth. Out the door he went and over to the edge of the curb, set his feet on the edge, leaned over and cleared both nostrils. Splat! Splat!

"You got to promise that you won't tell anyone. I want it to be a surprise. Hey, you listening?"

"Won't tell a soul, Joe, just the folks ... I promise."

"You guys got some sort of special sign?"

"Huh?"

"You know ... some sign that means you gave your word and that you'll die rather than talk?"

"Joe!"

"No sign, huh?"

"You got my word!"

"Okay ... you got a pen?"

Joe fumbled in his pockets and came up with a grocery receipt from the Green Front. He looked over the top of the booth and all around the coffee shop and then wrote something on the receipt. It was so small you could hardly read it.

"Math ... Mathe ... ah ... Lar ... Ler ... Lerzo ..."

"Matthew Larson," shouted Joe.

"Matthew Larson?"

Joe was nodding his head up and down and smiling like a big kid.

"Matthew Larson ... the lumber magnate? The Matthew Larson who built the mansion over on Bay Street?"

"Shsssssss, damn, keep your voice down. Dingdang, you talk loud!"

"The pageant is going to be about him?"

"Founder of this town. Make a great pageant. I'm going to call it 'Matthew Larson and the Deer Island Massacre.'"

"Deer Island Massacre?"

"Never heard of it, right? Course you haven't. Can't read or write. I'll bet not many people in this town know about it. Happened in 1863. Larson and his two brothers brought a boat up from San Francisco and dropped anchor in the bay. Nothing here then but the salt flats and the bay and the trees and some Indians."

"Thirty or forty Indians?"

"Right ... and within four months Larson had brought up about fifty families. Part of them began logging the timber and setting up a mill, the others began to build the town. Some of the families including Larson and his brothers moved over to Deer Island where the marina is now. There was a band of Indians on the island and relations between Larson and the chief didn't go too well. Hey, you still awake?"

"Deer Island, huh?"

"Right. And in the middle of the night on March 31, 1863, just a bit after midnight, the massacre took place."

"Massacre?"

"Keep your voice down! Damn! Yes, a massacre. Larson's two brothers were killed but Larson survived and built the town. That's how this place was started. Make a good pageant, huh?"

"And you want me to get you Indians to play the part of the Indians on Deer Island ... the ones involved in the massacre?"

"What else would I want Indians for?"

"Joe ... I'm not sure I can do that ... I mean ... you know my folks ... they may not like ..."

"What's to like? It's all history. You can't muck around with history. It ain't always the way we'd like it to be but there it is. Can't change it."

"But Joe ..."

"Dingdang, now don't go getting huffy and sulky on me, Chief. I need thirty or forty Indians and you said you could get them. It'll make a great pageant."

"Who gets to play Matthew Larson?"

"Well, you sure as hell can't play Larson. Larson was a whiteman. You don't look like a whiteman. You look like an Indian. I'll probably play Larson."

Confidence, that's what Joe had, and civic pride. Sure enough, at the end of the month, Joe called me up and yelled over the phone that his idea was one of the three that had been chosen and that Mayor Anderson had caught Joe after the meeting and told him how much he liked Joe's idea.

"Great idea, Joe, that's what he said. Shook my hand, bought me a cup of coffee from that machine they have. Awful damn coffee. I told him, too ... awful damn coffee."

"Chief, they liked the idea so much, I didn't even have to show them my script."

"You got a script?"

"Damn if you're not blind and deaf! Course I got a script. I just don't want to show it to every nosepusher that comes heeltoeing up. I want it to be a surprise. Everyone'll see it at the competition. Say ... did you get me those Indians?"

Folks at the Bar said sure, they'd come ... be kinda fun. My aunts at Round Valley said yes, too, and Bernie and James over at Hupa promised to come and bring as many of their friends and neighbors as they could find.

"Where we going to put the folks during the rehearsals?"

"That's the best part. The mayor said that the Indians could pitch their tents on Deer Island."

"I don't know if they have tents, Joe."

"The hell you say!"

"I'll see what I can do."

"The mayor said they could use the facilities at the marina. And Chief ... you listening, Chief ... rehearsals begin on Monday."

Rehearsals began on Friday. My father couldn't make it down from the Bar right away and Aunt Amy and her girls had car trouble in Laytonville and had to wait there two days for a part. Bernie and James and about ten of their relations came down to the island to say hi and then disappeared in town. Just as well, too. It took the mayor until Wednesday to find enough tents and butane stoves. Even Joe wasn't ready ... some last minute changes to the script. By Thursday night the camp was set up and everyone was there.

"Ho," said my father, looking around the camp and smiling, "just like the old days."

Around ten o'clock that evening Joe came bustling into camp with a cardboard box that said Seagram's on the side. I knew it wasn't liquor but Bernie and James were disappointed when Joe opened the box and took out a few scripts.

"Howdy," said Joe and he shook hands and introduced himself to everyone in the camp including the kids. "Thanks for coming. Real good of you to come. It's going to be a great pageant."

"Why's he shouting?" said Bernie.

"These are the scripts. I don't know most of you so I'm going to let the Chief here hand out the parts."

Everyone sort of looked around casual-like and skinnied their necks to see who Joe was talking about.

"Hey ... is he talking about you, cousin?" And James began to laugh.

"You must have gotten a promotion that we didn't hear about over in the valley."

"Floyd, hey, Floyd ... give us an honor song for the Chief here."

Joe just grinned and dropped the box of scripts in my lap.

"Tomorrow," he shouted, "we start tomorrow."

That first night on Deer Island was soft and quiet. Some of us got propped up against the tight clusters of marsh grass and listened to my father and my uncles tell stories. All the kids were sprawled on top of one another like a litter of puppies. After the men got things going, Aunt Amy took over. She was the best storyteller. Bernie and James got out a drum and started singing a few social songs and some of the families danced for a while. Mostly we watched the fires and watched the fog slip in off the mud flats and curl around the tents. You could hear the frogs in the distance and the water pushing at the edges of the island. As I went to sleep, I imagined that in the morning, when the fog lifted, the town and the pulp factory and the marina and Larson's mansion would be gone and all you'd be able to see was the flats stretched out to the trees.

I didn't read the script until early the next morning.

"Ho," said my father, "did you read this?"

"Joe did a lot of research on it." And that was all I could think of saying.

"Son, you better talk to Joe."

"Sure, I'll talk to Joe."

Damn, if there wasn't going to be trouble.

"What'd you think of the script?" Joe shouted.

"Joe ..."

"Told you I could write."

"Joe ..."

"Typed it myself, too!"

"Joe ..."

"Had to go all the way to Sacramento for some of the old records."

"Damn it, Joe ..."

"No sense in talking about it. Got just enough time to get it together. Come on. Dingdang, time's halfway to China ... round up your Indians and let's get started."

"Did you talk to Joe?"

"Sure, dad ... I talked to Joe."

"What did he say?"

"He said we needed to get started."

"Ho."

Joe had us practice every day. We ran up and down the sand, yelling and hollering and rolling around in the marsh grass.

At the end of the first week, Joe backed me up against one of the tents and lowered his voice.

"Chief, we got a little problem."

"A problem?"

"Your Indians don't look like Indians."

"What?"

"Now, don't take offense. I know they're Indians ... you're not one to slip in a few Italians or Chinese on me but they don't look like Indians."

"Joe ..."

"Bothered you too, I know ... couldn't put my finger on it at first but now I got it. None of your folks have got long hair."

"Long hair?"

"They all got crew cuts! Hell, we can't have Indians with crew cuts. No one's going to believe that Indians in 1863 had crew cuts. They got to have long hair with braids ... everybody. We got to find them some wigs."

"Wigs?"

"No time to grow long hair. You got any ideas? You're sure easy with the questions."

"I don't know ... maybe the drama department at the high school would have some wigs."

"Now you're talking."

The drama department only had ten wigs and they didn't much look like Indian wigs but Joe said that they'd do. Lucille's dress shop loaned us another eight ... off their manikins. Bernie got twelve balls of black yarn from a yard sale. Aunt Amy and her girls and a bunch of the boys braided the yarn into braids. If you wore a hat, you could stuff the braids along the side and they looked pretty good. But we were still short about ten wigs.

"Not to worry," shouted Joe, slapping his head with inspiration. "The rest of the Indians can play the parts of Larson and his brothers and the other men."

I got to admit that putting on the pageant was fun. The kids had a great time there on the island and the evenings got better and better. Towards the end, some of the folks from the town came on over and sat around and talked. A few even got up and danced. Dad took old Mrs. Pearson and danced her around for near a half hour.

Boy, were we nervous on the day of the competition.

"You all know your parts," Joe shouted and he shouted even louder than usual.

"Damn," said James, "that man can shout."

"No point in being anxious. You'll do a great job. Just remember to yell like hell. Make it look real."

We were the last group to perform. The first pageant was pretty good. It was about Sarah Jute and the 1903 fire. Fire started in Pearson's warehouse on New Year's Eve. Most of the firemen were at a party and pretty drunk. Sarah was a prostitute in Old Town. New Year's Eve was a busy time for her, but when she saw the fire, she rounded up the rest of her friends and some of the men who were with them and they all formed a bucket line and held the fire in check until help arrived. Sally Jamison played the lead. She was great as Sarah, running up and down the line, yelling instructions to the women ... real energetic.

"Hey," I said to Joe, "that was pretty good."

The second pageant was real dull. Paul Wolwik had gotten some of the businessmen together to act out the founding of the first city council. We all clapped to be polite.

Then it was our turn.

"Okay, Chief, let's knock them to their legs."

"Pretty good crowd, huh, Joe?"

The city council had set up about fifty chairs along the boardwalk of the marina. The mayor and his wife were right in the middle. But there were a lot more people than there were chairs and the rest of the folk were either leaning against the railing or dug into comfortable positions in the sand.

"You nervous, Joe?"

"Dingdang!"

Joe put on his hat and walked out through the sand. He had on a black frock coat that the high school had loaned us and a broad brimmed black hat. He looked impressive in the coat and the vest with the gold watch chain strung from pocket to pocket. He didn't have a watch though. The chain was hooked around a couple of flat washers so it wouldn't fall out. Matthew Larson couldn't have looked grander.

"The pageant that the Native Sons Players are about to present," Joe began in a thunderous voice, "is about the founding of our town. It is about our founder, Matthew Larson, and how he came to Sequoia County in 1863 and sculptured a town out of a barren wilderness. I hope you all enjoy the weather and our presentation."

Native Sons Players! Damn, that Joe was creative. Sounded professional.

The pageant was in three parts. The first part dramatized Matthew Larson landing near Rocky Point and coming ashore. He was greeted by an Indian named Redbird who lived with his tribe on Deer Island.

I got to play Redbird.

Larson and Redbird greeted one another and Redbird invited Larson back to his camp. Redbird gave Larson some otter skins and Larson gave Redbird a couple of iron kettles and a Bible. The two men parted friends and Larson returned to San Francisco to get the rest of his family and friends.

I didn't forget any of my lines. No one had any trouble hearing Joe. At the end of the first act, everyone clapped. Mayor Anderson clapped really hard and smiled at everyone around him.

The second act started with the arrival of Larson and the other people. My two uncles from the Bar and their families and three or four of the folks from Hupa played the parts of the settlers. Everyone ran around pretending like they were building a town. Halfway through the act, I came out to complain that Larson and his people were encroaching on my people's land. I thought it sounded strange for an Indian in 1863 to complain about Whites "encroaching" on their land but Joe swore that it was a direct quote from the historical record. Redbird had a better vocabulary than I did.

"God gave this land for all to use, Red and White," shouted Joe.

"We will share it with you, whiteman," I said with my arms folded across my chest like Joe showed me, "but you must not build your houses on our island. My people live there and we are happy."

You could see the tension building.

The second act ended with Matthew Larson and his two brothers coming ashore at Deer Island and claiming that it belonged to them. I had a nice monologue at the end of the second act.

"The whiteman takes more than he needs. He is greedy like a bear in the spring. We will share the forest and the rivers and the great lake but we will not share this island. It is our home. We will fight to keep it. Beware, whiteman, the wrath of the Indian is swift and terrible."

There was a short break between the second and third act so that the people in the audience could stretch and so that us actors could get ready for the last act.

"The year is 1863," Joe shouted. "Matthew Larson has defied Redbird and ignored his warning. Larson and his brothers have landed on Deer Island and have begun to build homes for themselves and their families. Redbird and his people are camped nearby."

That was our cue. Everybody came trooping out to the center of the island right in front of where the mayor and the council were sitting. Aunt Amy and the girls built a fire and we all got into our positions.

"It is evening," Joe continued, "and the Indians are singing and dancing around the fire."

"Hey, ah, ah, ah, ah ... ahhha," Bernie began the song nice and loud so everyone could hear and then the rest of us joined in. It sounded pretty fierce but it was just one of the 49ers that Bernie and the rest of us knew. Some of the kids were singing along and dancing and trying to keep those yarn braids under their hats.

"The Indians were dancing and singing and you could hear

the drum and the bloodcurdling shouts all the way up the island where Matthew Larson and his family huddled in their houses."

And that was our cue to sing real loud and whoop and jump around on the sand. James and his cousins were really getting into it.

"Damn," said James as he fancy-danced past me, "this is fun."

"But the night grew late," Joe bellowed above the drum and the singing, "and the Indians grew tired. Soon they were all asleep, tired out from all the dancing and singing."

We all began to yawn and stretch and say things like, "Boy, I'm tired," but we said them in Cherokee or Hupa so that the crowd didn't know. One of my uncles told a pretty bad joke and some of the kids began to laugh. We stretched out on the sand and pretended to be asleep.

"It is now about midnight," Joe shouted at the crowd, "and the pale moon is hidden by the fog that has stolen out of the bay. And in the distance, if you listen very carefully, you can hear the muffled sound of oars."

I opened one eye so I could see what was going on. Joe bowed to the crowd and trudged off across the sand. He waved to the mayor as he disappeared under the boardwalk and the mayor waved back. In a minute, Joe reappeared with Uncle Ben and some of the men from the Bar and a few of the older kids. They were dressed in jeans and jackets 'cause we couldn't find any good costumes for all of them. But they all had rifles and knives and Uncle Ben had an old sword that he had borrowed from Captain Oleg, who ran a salmon charter for the tourists during the summer.

They all came creeping across the sand real quiet. When

they were about thirty feet away, Joe stood up and said in a loud voice that we weren't supposed to hear:

"There's their camp, men. Spread out and let none escape. It's God's work ... there'll be no peace with Redbird and his people for there can be no peace between Christians and heathens. Steel your hearts to the cries of the Indians. Who goes with me to make our families safe? Who goes with me to bring the light of civilization to this dark land?"

And Uncle Ben and the rest of the men shook their rifles and waved their knives and shouted, "We're with you, Matthew!"

"Then do your duty," yells Joe and all the men came charging into our camp.

"Whites!" yells one of the kids.

"We're being attacked," yells another.

"Grab your arms, men," I yell, leaping out of the sand. "Protect the women and children."

Jimmy Pete comes at me with a knife and I whack him with my tomahawk. Aunt Amy pushes Uncle Ben over a log and is then shot by Jesse Long from Hupa who is playing the part of Matthew's brother William. James shoots Jesse and Joe kills both Bernie and James.

We couldn't find any blanks for the guns so we just shout out, "Bang! Bang! Bang!" real loud.

It looks real good, too. Some of the kids got a bunch of little plastic bags of ketchup from Connie's restaurant. Blood. They hadn't worked very well at first 'cause they wouldn't break easily when you smashed them against your chest. But if you tore them open a bit, they worked fine. We taped one to each hand so that when we were shot, we could slap a hand over the wound and it looked like we had really been shot or stabbed.

"Death to the heathens," shouts Joe and he shoots me dead.

"I'm killed," I moan and slap a ketchup pack against my stomach. I have to do it twice. Those packets are tough.

"I'm dead," I say again. "Matthew Larson has killed me and all my people."

In a minute, all of us are lying in the sand trying to look dead. The flies start to buzz around the ketchup.

Everything was quiet. The mayor and the council just sat there. Joe took off his hat.

"I abhor the taking of a human life but civilization needs a strong arm to open the frontier. Farewell, Redman. Know that from your bones will spring a new and stronger community forever."

When the clapping started, we were all supposed to get up and take a bow.

But it didn't start. Everyone just sat there. The mayor was looking red and snapped around to whisper something to his wife.

Joe was kneeling next to me with his rifle.

"Just stay there," he said, "it'll take 'em a minute to warm to it. It was more powerful than I thought."

Then someone began to clap and everyone joined in. We got up and took our bows.

We stayed on Deer Island that night. The next morning James and Bernie and I packed up the tent and the wigs and the stoves and returned them. I didn't see Joe for three or four days. Word was that the mayor was upset and that he and Joe had had words and that Joe had taken the lion's share.

"Howdy Chief, you want some coffee?"

"Sure Joe, hell, where you been? My father said he really enjoyed that pageant. All the folks said to tell you if you need Indians again to just give them a call."

"That was a good pageant, wasn't it?"

"The best, Joe."

"The mayor didn't like it."

"What does he know."

"He said it wasn't apppprooooopriate!"

"What does he know."

"The committee chose Wolwik's pageant."

"What? What about Sally's pageant? That was better than Wolwik's."

And Joe began to laugh. God, that man could laugh louder than he could talk.

"The mayor said that Sally's pageant wasn't apppprooooopriate, either."

"Damn."

"Come on, I'll buy. I still got some of that pageant money left. We can get some pie, too ... à la mode."

Everyone in town knew Joe. And all the people who knew Joe as well as I knew Joe didn't like him. Except me.

I like Joe.

A Coyote
Columbus
Story

You know, Coyote came by my place the other day. She was going to a party. She had her party hat and she had her party whistle and she had her party rattle.

I'm going to a party, she says.

Yes, I says, I can see that.

It is a party for Christopher Columbus, says Coyote. That is the one who found America. That is the one who found Indians.

Boy, that Coyote is one silly Coyote. You got to watch out for her. Some of Coyote's stories have got Coyote tails and some of Coyote's stories are covered with scraggy Coyote fur but all of Coyote's stories are bent.

Christopher Columbus didn't find America, I says. Christopher Columbus didn't find Indians, either. You got a tail on that story.

Oh no, says Coyote. I read it in a book.

Must have been a Coyote book, I says.

No, no, no, no, says Coyote. It was a history book. Big red one. All about how Christopher Columbus sailed the ocean blue looking for America and the Indians.

Sit down, I says. Have some tea. We're going to have to do this story right. We're going to have to do this story now.

It was all Old Coyote's fault, I tell Coyote, and here is how the story goes. Here is what really happened.

So.

Old Coyote loved to play ball, you know. She played ball all day and all night. She would throw the ball and she would hit the ball and she would run and catch the ball. But playing ball by herself was boring, so she sang a song and she danced a dance and she thought about playing ball and pretty soon along came some Indians. Old Coyote and the Indians became very good friends. You are sure a good friend, says those Indians. Yes, that's true, says Old Coyote.

But, you know, whenever Old Coyote and the Indians played ball, Old Coyote always won. She always won because she made up the rules. That sneaky one made up the rules and she always won because she could do that.

That's not fair, says the Indians. Friends don't do that.

That's the rules, says Old Coyote. Let's play some more. Maybe you will win the next time. But they don't.

You keep changing the rules, says those Indians.

No, no, no, no, says Old Coyote. You are mistaken. And then she changes the rules again.

So, after a while, those Indians find better things to do.

Some of them go fishing.

Some of them go shopping.

Some of them go to a movie.

Some of them go on a vacation.

Those Indians got better things to do than play ball with Old Coyote and those changing rules.

So, Old Coyote doesn't have anyone to play with.

So, she has to play by herself.

So, she gets bored.

When Old Coyote gets bored, anything can happen. Stick around. Big trouble is coming, I can tell you that.

Well. That silly one sings a song and she dances a dance and she thinks about playing ball. But she's thinking about changing those rules, too, and she doesn't watch what she is making up out of her head. So pretty soon, she makes three ships.

Hmmmm, says Old Coyote, where did those ships come from?

And pretty soon, she makes some people on those ships.

Hmmmm, says Old Coyote, where did those people come from?

And pretty soon, she makes some people on the beach with flags and funny-looking clothes and stuff.

Hooray, says Old Coyote. You are just in time for the ball game.

Hello, says one of the men in silly clothes and red hair all over his head. I am Christopher Columbus. I am sailing the ocean blue looking for China. Have you seen it?

Forget China, says Old Coyote. Let's play ball.

It must be around here somewhere, says Christopher Columbus. I have a map.

Forget the map, says Old Coyote. I'll bat first and I'll tell you the rules as we go along.

But that Christopher Columbus and his friends don't want to play ball. We got work to do, he says. We got to find China. We got to find things we can sell.

Yes, says those Columbus people, where is the gold?

Yes, they says, where is that silk cloth?

Yes, they says, where are those portable color televisions?

Yes, they says, where are those home computers?

Boy, says Old Coyote, and that one scratches her head. I must have sung that song wrong. Maybe I didn't do the right dance. Maybe I thought too hard. These people I made have no manners. They act as if they have no relations.

And she is right. Christopher Columbus and his friends start jumping up and down in their funny clothes and they shout so loud that Coyote's ears almost fall off.

Boy, what a bunch of noise, says Coyote. What bad manners. You guys got to stop jumping and shouting or my ears will fall off.

We got to find China, says Christopher Columbus. We got to become rich. We got to become famous. Do you think you can help us?

But all Old Coyote can think about is playing ball.

I'll let you bat first, says Old Coyote.

No time for games, says Christopher Columbus.

I'll let you make the rules, cries Old Coyote.

But those Columbus people don't listen. They are too busy running around, peeking under rocks, looking in caves, sailing all over the place. Looking for China. Looking for stuff they can sell.

I got a monkey, says one.

I got a parrot, says another.

I got a fish, says a third.

I got a coconut, says a fourth.

That stuff isn't worth poop, says Christopher Columbus. We can't sell those things in Spain. Look harder.

But all they find are monkeys and parrots and fish and coconuts. And when they tell Christopher Columbus, that one he squeezes his ears and he chews his nose and grinds his teeth. He grinds his teeth so hard, he gets a headache, and, then, he gets cranky.

And then he gets an idea.

Say, says Christopher Columbus. Maybe we could sell Indians.

Yes, says his friends, that's a good idea. We could sell Indians, and they throw away their monkeys and parrots and fish and coconuts.

Wait a minute, says the Indians, that is not a good idea. That is a bad idea. That is a bad idea full of bad manners.

When Old Coyote hears this bad idea, she starts to laugh. Who would buy Indians, she says, and she laughs some more. She laughs so hard, she has to hold her nose on her face with both her hands.

But while that Old Coyote is laughing, Christopher Columbus grabs a big bunch of Indian men and Indian women and Indian children and locks them up in his ships.

When Old Coyote stops laughing and looks around, she sees that some of the Indians are missing. Hey, she says, where are those Indians? Where are my friends?

I'm going to sell them in Spain, says Christopher Columbus. Somebody has to pay for this trip. Sailing over the ocean blue isn't cheap, you know.

But Old Coyote still thinks that Christopher Columbus is playing a trick. She thinks it is a joke. That is a good joke, she says, trying to make me think that you are going to sell my friends. And she starts to laugh again.

Grab some more Indians, says Christopher Columbus.

When Old Coyote sees Christopher Columbus grab some more Indians, she laughs even harder. What a good joke, she says. And she laughs some more. She does this four times and when she is done laughing, all the Indians are gone. And Christopher Columbus is gone and Christopher Columbus's friends are gone, too.

Wait a minute, says old Coyote. What happened to my friends? Where are my Indians? You got to bring them back. Who's going to play ball with me?

But Christopher Columbus didn't bring the Indians back and Old Coyote was real sorry she thought him up. She tried to take him back. But, you know, once you think things like that, you can't take them back. So you have to be careful what you think.

So. That's the end of the story.

Boy, says Coyote. That is one sad story.

Yes, I says. It's sad alright. And things don't get any better, I can tell you that.

What a very sad story, says Coyote. Poor Old Coyote didn't have anyone to play ball with. That one must have been lonely. And Coyote begins to cry.

Stop crying, I says. Old Coyote is fine. Some blue jays come along after that and they play ball with her.

Oh, good, says Coyote. But what happened to the Indians? There was nothing in that red history book about Christopher Columbus and the Indians.

Christopher Columbus sold the Indians, I says, and that one became rich and famous.

Oh, good, says Coyote. I love a happy ending. And that one blows her party whistle and that one shakes her party rattle and that one puts her party hat back on her head. I better get going, she says, I'm going to be late for the party.

Okay, I says. Just remember how that story goes. Don't go messing it up again. Have you got it straight, now?

You bet, says Coyote. But if Christopher Columbus didn't find America and he didn't find Indians, who found these things?

Those things were never lost, I says. Those things were always here. Those things are still here today.

By golly, I think you are right, says Coyote.

Don't be thinking, I says. This world has enough problems already without a bunch of Coyote thoughts with tails and scraggy fur running around bumping into each other.

Boy, that's the truth. I can tell you that.

Borders

When I was twelve, maybe thirteen, my mother announced that we were going to go to Salt Lake City to visit my sister who had left the reserve, moved across the line, and found a job. Laetitia had not left home with my mother's blessing, but over time my mother had come to be proud of the fact that Laetitia had done all of this on her own.

"She did real good," my mother would say.

Then there were the fine points to Laetitia's going. She had not, as my mother liked to tell Mrs. Manyfingers, gone floating after some man like a balloon on a string. She hadn't snuck out of the house, either, and gone to Vancouver or Edmonton or Toronto to chase rainbows down alleys. And she hadn't been pregnant.

"She did real good."

I was seven or eight when Laetitia left home. She was seventeen. Our father was from Rocky Boy on the American side.

"Dad's American," Laetitia told my mother, "so I can go and come as I please."

"Send us a postcard."

Laetitia packed her things, and we headed for the border. Just outside of Milk River, Laetitia told us to watch for the water tower.

"Over the next rise. It's the first thing you see."

"We got a water tower on the reserve," my mother said. "There's a big one in Lethbridge, too."

"You'll be able to see the tops of the flagpoles, too. That's where the border is."

When we got to Coutts, my mother stopped at the convenience store and bought her and Laetitia a cup of coffee. I got an Orange Crush.

"This is real lousy coffee."

"You're just angry because I want to see the world."

"It's the water. From here on down, they got lousy water."

"I can catch the bus from Sweetgrass. You don't have to lift a finger."

"You're going to have to buy your water in bottles if you want good coffee."

There was an old wooden building about a block away, with a tall sign in the yard that said "Museum." Most of the roof had been blown away. Mom told me to go and see when the place was open. There were boards over the windows and doors. You could tell that the place was closed, and I told Mom so, but she said to go and check anyway. Mom and Laetitia stayed by the car. Neither one of them moved. I sat down on the steps of the museum and watched them, and I don't know that they ever said anything to each other. Finally, Laetitia got her bag out of the trunk and gave Mom a hug.

I wandered back to the car. The wind had come up, and it blew Laetitia's hair across her face. Mom reached out and pulled the strands out of Laetitia's eyes, and Laetitia let her.

"You can still see the mountain from here," my mother told Laetitia in Blackfoot.

"Lots of mountains in Salt Lake," Laetitia told her in English.

"The place is closed," I said. "Just like I told you."

Laetitia tucked her hair into her jacket and dragged her bag down the road to the brick building with the American flag flapping on a pole. When she got to where the guards were waiting, she turned, put the bag down, and waved to us. We waved back. Then my mother turned the car around, and we came home.

We got postcards from Laetitia regular, and, if she wasn't spreading jelly on the truth, she was happy. She found a good job and rented an apartment with a pool.

"And she can't even swim," my mother told Mrs. Manyfingers.

Most of the postcards said we should come down and see the city, but whenever I mentioned this, my mother would stiffen up.

So I was surprised when she bought two new tires for the car and put on her blue dress with the green and yellow flowers. I had to dress up, too, for my mother did not want us crossing the border looking like Americans. We made sandwiches and put them in a big box with pop and potato chips and some apples and bananas and a big jar of water.

"But we can stop at one of those restaurants, too, right?"

"We maybe should take some blankets in case you get sleepy."

"But we can stop at one of those restaurants, too, right?"

The border was actually two towns, though neither one was big enough to amount to anything. Coutts was on the

Canadian side and consisted of the convenience store and gas station, the museum that was closed and boarded up, and a motel. Sweetgrass was on the American side, but all you could see was an overpass that arched across the highway and disappeared into the prairies. Just hearing the names of these towns, you would expect that Sweetgrass, which is a nice name and sounds like it is related to other places such as Medicine Hat and Moose Jaw and Kicking Horse Pass, would be on the Canadian side, and that Coutts, which sounds abrupt and rude, would be on the American side. But this was not the case.

Between the two borders was a duty-free shop where you could buy cigarettes and liquor and flags. Stuff like that.

We left the reserve in the morning and drove until we got to Coutts.

"Last time we stopped here," my mother said, "you had an Orange Crush. You remember that?"

"Sure," I said. "That was when Laetitia took off."

"You want another Orange Crush?"

"That means we're not going to stop at a restaurant, right?"

My mother got a coffee at the convenience store, and we stood around and watched the prairies move in the sunlight. Then we climbed back in the car. My mother straightened the dress across her thighs, leaned against the wheel, and drove all the way to the border in first gear, slowly, as if she were trying to see through a bad storm or riding high on black ice.

The border guard was an old guy. As he walked to the car, he swayed from side to side, his feet set wide apart, the holster on his hip pitching up and down. He leaned into the window, looked into the back seat, and looked at my mother and me.

"Morning, ma'am."

"Good morning."

"Where you heading?"

"Salt Lake City."

"Purpose of your visit?"

"Visit my daughter."

"Citizenship?"

"Blackfoot," my mother told him.

"Ma'am?"

"Blackfoot," my mother repeated.

"Canadian?"

"Blackfoot."

It would have been easier if my mother had just said "Canadian" and been done with it, but I could see she wasn't going to do that. The guard wasn't angry or anything. He smiled and looked towards the building. Then he turned back and nodded.

"Morning, ma'am."

"Good morning."

"Any firearms or tobacco?"

"No."

"Citizenship?"

"Blackfoot."

He told us to sit in the car and wait, and we did. In about five minutes, another guard came out with the first man. They were talking as they came, both men swaying back and forth like two cowboys headed for a bar or a gunfight.

"Morning, ma'am."

"Good morning."

"Cecil tells me you and the boy are Blackfoot."

"That's right."

"Now, I know that we got Blackfeet on the American side

and the Canadians got Blackfeet on their side. Just so we can keep our records straight, what side do you come from?"

I knew exactly what my mother was going to say, and I could have told them if they had asked me.

"Canadian side or American side?" asked the guard.

"Blackfoot side," she said.

It didn't take them long to lose their sense of humor, I can tell you that. The one guard stopped smiling altogether and told us to park our car at the side of the building and come in.

We sat on a wood bench for about an hour before anyone came over to talk to us. This time it was a woman. She had a gun, too.

"Hi," she said. "I'm Inspector Pratt. I understand there is a little misunderstanding."

"I'm going to visit my daughter in Salt Lake City," my mother told her. "We don't have any guns or beer."

"It's a legal technicality, that's all."

"My daughter's Blackfoot, too."

The woman opened a briefcase and took out a couple of forms and began to write on one of them. "Everyone who crosses our border has to declare their citizenship. Even Americans. It helps us keep track of the visitors we get from the various countries."

She went on like that for maybe fifteen minutes, and a lot of the stuff she told us was interesting.

"I can understand how you feel about having to tell us your citizenship, and here's what I'll do. You tell me, and I won't put it down on the form. No-one will know but you and me."

Her gun was silver. There were several chips in the wood handle and the name "Stella" was scratched into the metal butt.

We were in the border office for about four hours, and we talked to almost everyone there. One of the men bought me a Coke. My mother brought a couple of sandwiches in from the car. I offered part of mine to Stella, but she said she wasn't hungry.

I told Stella that we were Blackfoot and Canadian, but she said that that didn't count because I was a minor. In the end, she told us that if my mother didn't declare her citizenship, we would have to go back to where we came from. My mother stood up and thanked Stella for her time. Then we got back in the car and drove to the Canadian border, which was only about a hundred yards away.

I was disappointed. I hadn't seen Laetitia for a long time, and I had never been to Salt Lake City. When she was still at home, Laetitia would go on and on about Salt Lake City. She had never been there, but her boyfriend Lester Tallbull had spent a year in Salt Lake at a technical school.

"It's a great place," Lester would say. "Nothing but blondes in the whole state."

Whenever he said that, Laetitia would slug him on his shoulder hard enough to make him flinch. He had some brochures on Salt Lake and some maps, and every so often the two of them would spread them out on the table.

"That's the temple. It's right downtown. You got to have a pass to get in."

"Charlotte says anyone can go in and look around."

"When was Charlotte in Salt Lake? Just when the hell was Charlotte in Salt Lake?"

"Last year."

"This is Liberty Park. It's got a zoo. There's good skiing in the mountains."

"Got all the skiing we can use," my mother would say. "People come from all over the world to ski at Banff. Cardston's got a temple, if you like those kinds of things."

"Oh, this one is real big," Lester would say. "They got armed guards and everything."

"Not what Charlotte says."

"What does she know?"

Lester and Laetitia broke up, but I guess the idea of Salt Lake stuck in her mind.

The Canadian border guard was a young woman, and she seemed happy to see us. "Hi," she said. "You folks sure have a great day for a trip. Where are you coming from?"

"Standoff."

"Is that in Montana?"

"No."

"Where are you going?"

"Standoff."

The woman's name was Carol and I don't guess she was any older than Laetitia. "Wow, you both Canadians?"

"Blackfoot."

"Really? I have a friend I went to school with who is Blackfoot. Do you know Mike Harley?"

"No."

"He went to school in Lethbridge, but he's really from Browning."

It was a nice conversation and there were no cars behind us, so there was no rush.

"You're not bringing any liquor back, are you?"

"No."

"Any cigarettes or plants or stuff like that?"

"No."

"Citizenship?"

"Blackfoot."

"I know," said the woman, "and I'd be proud of being Blackfoot if I were Blackfoot. But you have to be American or Canadian."

When Laetitia and Lester broke up, Lester took his brochures and maps with him, so Laetitia wrote to someone in Salt Lake City, and, about a month later, she got a big envelope of stuff. We sat at the table and opened up all the brochures, and Laetitia read each one out loud.

"Salt Lake City is the gateway to some of the world's most magnificent skiing.

"Salt Lake City is the home of one of the newest professional basketball franchises, the Utah Jazz.

"The Great Salt Lake is one of the natural wonders of the world."

It was kind of exciting seeing all those color brochures on the table and listening to Laetitia read all about how Salt Lake City was one of the best places in the entire world.

"That Salt Lake City place sounds too good to be true," my mother told her.

"It has everything."

"We got everything right here."

"It's boring here."

"People in Salt Lake City are probably sending away for brochures of Calgary and Lethbridge and Pincher Creek right now."

In the end, my mother would say that maybe Laetitia should go to Salt Lake City, and Laetitia would say that maybe she would.

We parked the car to the side of the building and Carol led us into a small room on the second floor. I found a comfortable spot on the couch and flipped through some back issues of *Saturday Night* and *Alberta Report*.

When I woke up, my mother was just coming out of another office. She didn't say a word to me. I followed her down the stairs and out to the car. I thought we were going home, but she turned the car around and drove back towards the American border, which made me think we were going to visit Laetitia in Salt Lake City after all. Instead she pulled into the parking lot of the duty-free store and stopped.

"We going to see Laetitia?"

"No."

"We going home?"

Pride is a good thing to have, you know. Laetitia had a lot of pride, and so did my mother. I figured that someday, I'd have it, too.

"So where are we going?"

Most of that day, we wandered around the duty-free store, which wasn't very large. The manager had a name tag with a tiny American flag on one side and a tiny Canadian flag on the other. His name was Mel. Towards evening, he began suggesting that we should be on our way. I told him we had nowhere to go, that neither the Americans nor the Canadians would let us in. He laughed at that and told us that we should buy something or leave.

The car was not very comfortable, but we did have all that

food and it was April, so even if it did snow as it sometimes does on the prairies, we wouldn't freeze. The next morning my mother drove to the American border.

It was a different guard this time, but the questions were the same. We didn't spend as much time in the office as we had the day before. By noon, we were back at the Canadian border. By two we were back in the duty-free shop parking lot.

The second night in the car was not as much fun as the first, but my mother seemed in good spirits, and, all in all, it was as much an adventure as an inconvenience. There wasn't much food left and that was a problem, but we had lots of water as there was a faucet at the side of the duty-free shop.

One Sunday, Laetitia and I were watching television. Mom was over at Mrs. Manyfingers's. Right in the middle of the program, Laetitia turned off the set and said she was going to Salt Lake City, that life around here was too boring. I had wanted to see the rest of the program and really didn't care if Laetitia went to Salt Lake City or not. When Mom got home, I told her what Laetitia had said.

What surprised me was how angry Laetitia got when she found out that I had told Mom.

"You got a big mouth."

."That's what you said."

"What I said is none of your business."

"I didn't say anything."

"Well, I'm going for sure, now."

That weekend, Laetitia packed her bags, and we drove her to the border.

Mel turned out to be friendly. When he closed up for the night and found us still parked in the lot, he came over and asked us if our car was broken down or something. My mother thanked him for his concern and told him that we were fine, that things would get straightened out in the morning.

"You're kidding," said Mel. "You'd think they could handle the simple things."

"We got some apples and a banana," I said, "but we're all out of ham sandwiches."

"You know, you read about these things, but you just don't believe it. You just don't believe it."

"Hamburgers would be even better because they got more stuff for energy."

My mother slept in the back seat. I slept in the front because I was smaller and could lie under the steering wheel. Late that night, I heard my mother open the car door. I found her sitting on her blanket leaning against the bumper of the car.

"You see all those stars," she said. "When I was a little girl, my grandmother used to take me and my sisters out on the prairies and tell us stories about all the stars."

"Do you think Mel is going to bring us any hamburgers?"

"Every one of those stars has a story. You see that bunch of stars over there that look like a fish?"

"He didn't say no."

"Coyote went fishing, one day. That's how it all started." We sat out under the stars that night, and my mother told me all sorts of stories. She was serious about it, too. She'd tell them slow, repeating parts as she went, as if she expected me to remember each one.

Early the next morning, the television vans began to arrive, and guys in suits and women in dresses came trotting over to us, dragging microphones and cameras and lights behind them. One of the vans had a table set up with orange juice and sandwiches and fruit. It was for the crew, but when I told them we hadn't eaten for a while, a really skinny blonde woman told us we could eat as much as we wanted.

They mostly talked to my mother. Every so often one of the reporters would come over and ask me questions about how it felt to be an Indian without a country. I told them we had a nice house on the reserve and that my cousins had a couple of horses we rode when we went fishing. Some of the television people went over to the American border, and then they went to the Canadian border.

Around noon, a good-looking guy in a dark blue suit and an orange tie with little ducks on it drove up in a fancy car. He talked to my mother for a while, and, after they were done talking, my mother called me over, and we got into our car. Just as my mother started the engine, Mel came over and gave us a bag of peanut brittle and told us that justice was a damn hard thing to get, but that we shouldn't give up.

I would have preferred lemon drops, but it was nice of Mel anyway.

"Where are we going now?"

"Going to visit Laetitia."

The guard who came out to our car was all smiles. The television lights were so bright they hurt my eyes, and, if you tried to look through the windshield in certain directions, you couldn't see a thing.

"Morning, ma'am."

"Good morning."

"Where you heading?"

"Salt Lake City."

"Purpose of your visit?"

"Visit my daughter."

"Any tobacco, liquor, or firearms?"

"Don't smoke."

"Any plants or fruit?"

"Not any more."

"Citizenship?"

"Blackfoot."

The guard rocked back on his heels and jammed his thumbs into his gun belt. "Thank you," he said, his fingers patting the butt of the revolver. "Have a pleasant trip."

My mother rolled the car forward, and the television people had to scramble out of the way. They ran alongside the car as we pulled away from the border, and, when they couldn't run any farther, they stood in the middle of the highway and waved and waved and waved.

We got to Salt Lake City the next day. Laetitia was happy to see us, and, that first night, she took us out to a restaurant that made really good soups. The list of pies took up a whole page. I had cherry. Mom had chocolate. Laetitia said that she saw us on television the night before and, during the meal, she had us tell her the story over and over again.

Laetitia took us everywhere. We went to a fancy ski resort. We went to the temple. We got to go shopping in a couple of large malls, but they weren't as large as the one in Edmonton, and Mom said so.

After a week or so, I got bored and wasn't at all sad when my mother said we should be heading back home. Laetitia wanted us to stay longer, but Mom said no, that she had things to do back home and that, next time, Laetitia should come up and visit. Laetitia said she was thinking about moving back, and Mom told her to do as she pleased, and Laetitia said that she would.

On the way home, we stopped at the duty-free shop, and my mother gave Mel a green hat that said "Salt Lake" across the front. Mel was a funny guy. He took the hat and blew his nose and told my mother that she was an inspiration to us all. He gave us some more peanut brittle and came out into the parking lot and waved at us all the way to the Canadian border.

It was almost evening when we left Coutts. I watched the border through the rear window until all you could see were the tops of the flagpoles and the blue water tower, and then they rolled over a hill and disappeared.

The stories in this collection appeared in earlier form
in the following publications:

"One Good Story, That One," *The Malahat Review,*
no. 82 (Spring 1988).

"Totem," *Whetstone* (Fall 1988).

"Magpies," *The Last Map Is the Heart* (Saskatoon:
Thistledown Press Ltd., 1989).

"Trap Lines," *Prism International* (July 1990).

"How Corporal Colin Sterling Saved Blossom, Alberta,
and Most of the Rest of the World as Well,"
Whetstone (Spring 1987).

"The One About Coyote Going West," *The Journal
of Wild Culture* (Fall 1989).

"A Seat in the Garden," *Books in Canada* (December 1990).

"Joe the Painter and the Deer Island Massacre,"
Whetstone (Spring 1985).

"A Coyote Columbus Story," originally published in a
different form by Groundwood Books Limited as *A Coyote
Columbus Story* with illustrations by Kent Monkman (1992).

"Borders," *Saturday Night* (December 1991).

Thomas King is an award-winning novelist, short story writer, scriptwriter, and photographer. His many books include *Medicine River, Truth and Bright Water, The Truth About Stories* (Minnesota, 2005), *A Short History of Indians in Canada* (Minnesota, 2013), and *The Inconvenient Indian: A Curious Account of Native People in North America* (Minnesota, 2013). He is the author of several picture books for children, the editor of *All My Relations: An Anthology of Contemporary Canadian Native Fiction,* and coeditor of *The Native in Literature: Canadian and Comparative Perspectives.* He has a popular CBC Radio series, *The Dead Dog Café Hour.* He is professor of English at the University of Guelph, where he teaches Native literature and creative writing.